THE
GURKHA'S
DAUGHTER

Quercus

New York • London

© 2013 by Prajwal Parajuly
Maps © 2013 by Raymond Turvey
First published in the United States by Quercus in 2014

ISBN 978-1-62365-145-9

Library of Congress Control Number: 2013913494

Distributed in the United States and Canada by
Random House Publisher Services
c/o Random House, 1745 Broadway
New York, NY 10019

Manufactured in the United States

10 9 8 7 6 5 4 3 2 1

www.quercus.com

THE
GURKHA'S
DAUGHTER

**PRAJWAL
PARAJULY**

Quercus

New York • London

To Shivabhakta Sharma (1918–2009) of Chiuribotey Busty,
Kalimpong, the best storyteller of them all

Contents

AUTHOR'S NOTE

The Gurkha's Daughter is an unusual title for a book published in North America. The word *Gurkha* in the title refers to a Nepalese soldier in the British Army. After the North American rights to the book were sold, the first question I asked my publishers at Quercus was if the title in the US and Canada would remain the same. After all, North Americans might not have the same familiarity with—or fondness for—these soldiers whom the United Kingdom and many other nations of the world associate with valiance. *Gurkha* was too foreign, too esoteric, too difficult on the tongue, I reasoned. *No Land Is Her Land* became a contender for the title, as did *The Cleft*. A few discussions later, however, we decided to stick with *The Gurkha's Daughter*—changing the name of the book just because it contained a foreign word, we concluded, would be underestimating the worldliness of the North American reader. In addition, the other titles didn't capture the inherent Nepaliness of the book (the term *Gurkha* is also increasingly being used to describe the Indian Nepalese) as perfectly as *The Gurkha's Daughter* did.

Gurkha is the anglicized version of *Gorkha*, which is the preferred spelling in South Asia. For more insight into the Nepalese words and phrases in the book, please consult the glossary. Since words may have different meanings depending on their context, some of the same words appear more than once across the glossary.

THE CLEFT

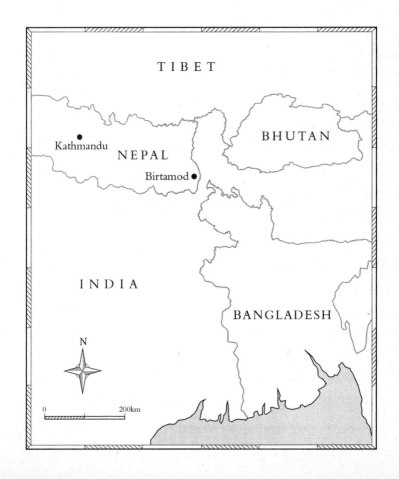

When Parvati first heard the news, by way of a phone call from her youngest brother-in-law in Birtamod, she applied some coconut oil to her hair and called for the servant girl to massage her scalp and temples. The two perched themselves on the rickety wooden stairs leading to the house, Parvati with her legs wide apart, as the servant's fingers adroitly negotiated their way through the thick tangle of hair on Parvati's head.

"The demon," Parvati said, smiling to herself. "She's dead."

"She's dead," the girl echoed.

"Do you even know who I am talking about, you foolish girl?" Parvati gently hit the servant's hand.

"Yes, your mother."

"Not my mother, but my mother-in-law. Your name is Kaali, you dark girl, and your brain is as dark as your face. You understand nothing."

"But you call her Aamaa, don't you?"

"Of course, I have to. What else would I call my husband's mother? My daughter? It's a good thing you've found employment here, Kaali. With the way you think, you'd be thrown out of everywhere else. Not to forget the way you look—black as coal and those grotesque lips. Were my husband alive, he'd have kicked you out already."

Parvati turned back to look at the servant's lip. Kaali's teeth protruded from under the cleft, and she looked like a mouse ready to nibble on a piece of cheese. Parvati touched the deformity with her fingers.

"Does it hurt?" she asked.

"No, I am used to it."

"That's the reason you still have a home, Kaali—you never complain. You wash plates like a blind woman—just today I had to rewash three plates—and you mop like a baby. You aren't good at anything and look like that, but I'll put up with you because of your attitude."

Kaali was now forming slow circles around Parvati's temples. Parvati's hair glistened in the Kathmandu sun, which was frail and playing hide-and-seek, and she let out a cry when Kaali, through a rough motion of fingers, selected a strand of gray hair and, pinching it between her thumb and forefinger, extracted a big, fat louse.

"Look at it," Kaali said, showing Parvati the insect crawling in between the lines of her palm. "That's a *dhaarey*. It sucks more blood than a *jumraa*."

Kaali threw the louse on the ground and, before it could escape, brought her thumb down to crush it, causing a tiny speck of blood to flick up and catch her cleft.

"I don't know where I've been getting these from," Parvati remarked. "It must be because I tie my hair right after washing it."

"These things thrive in damp hair," Kaali said.

"You know everything, don't you?"

"I don't see another one."

"You know what they say—when you see one, you don't see hundreds."

"I don't see any more of them."

"That's because you can't do anything efficiently, didn't I tell you?" Parvati said, adding in a resigned voice, "Maybe it is Aamaa's spirit."

"When will you go to Birtamod?" Kaali asked.

"Why? So you can watch TV all day? Think I don't know what you do when I am gone?"

"No, no, I just want to know. When will you go?"

"I am mourning right now," Parvati said with a wry smile. "I can't think straight. I am sure the relatives will come up with some plan for me."

"Will I go too?"

"Why? You want a plane ride, you greedy girl?"

"I didn't know we'd take a plane."

"There probably are no plane tickets available for today or tomorrow. Or the day after. The *bokshee* makes everything difficult. A woman who so easily made our lives difficult when alive is equally bad dead."

"Do you think she can hear us?"

"Let her, I don't care. But you haven't said anything bad about her, so why do you worry? If her *aatmaa* is still hovering around here, I'll be the one it will come to scare in the night. Your face would scare even the ghosts. Are you fourteen yet, Kaali?"

"Thirteen."

"If you stay with us for four more years, maybe we'll arrange for some surgery. Will that make you happy?"

"And school?" She spotted another louse but didn't pursue it.

"Why go to school?" Parvati looked straight at Kaali. "Look, I am high school pass, and yet I stay at home doing nothing. You need not go to school. Learn the basics from me. Show some initiative. Bring your notebook and pencil when I am free. But why would you? You're too busy running around Battisputalli with the neighborhood children, too busy imagining what a beauty you will turn into after the surgery. Remember, the surgery only takes place after four years, and I shall take into account every misbehavior of yours before I decide on it."

Yes, we will take care of the lip, he had said. *And school, too. Now that you talk to me about going to school, it seems you have a brain we can't waste, we shouldn't waste. It's just that all the mind-numbing chores at your mistress's place have made you rusty.*

The phone in the hallway put a stop to Kaali's daydream.

"Go get it," Parvati ordered. "The relatives must have made some travel arrangements. If anyone asks for me, tell them I am crying."

"What if they want to talk to you?"

"Tell them I can't talk."

Kaali ran to the phone while Parvati followed to listen in on the extension.

"Hello, Bhauju," the voice on the other end said. It was Sarita, Parvati's dead husband's sister.

"No, this is Kaali."

The voice at once changed. "Where's Bhauju?"

"She's crying."

"Call her."

"I can't. She's crying."

"I don't care. Call her to the phone. It's my mother who's dead, not hers, and I am not crying."

"She says no."

"You're so stupid. Are you the one with the bad lip?"

"Yes."

"Anyway, tell Bhauju to be ready. My brother-in-law has agreed to loan us his van and driver to go to Birtamod. There's a seat left for Bhauju. Her share will be two thousand rupees."

"What about me?"

"What will you do at a funeral? You can stay at home, or if you're that desperate, you can come sit in the trunk of the van with the luggage. It's a long journey, but you might have more space back there than we will in the front. All right, we'll be there in an hour. Tell her to be ready."

"I will, but what if she's not willing to listen to me?"

"And you, please wipe that snot off your face and wear something clean. I want a clean skirt."

Kaali didn't have to tell her mistress about the chat. Parvati hobbled into the hallway, a traumatized look on her face.

"How dare she?" she hissed. "You're clean. We've taught you clean habits. Don't you bathe once and sometimes twice a week? And no one should comment on your bad lip. It's not your fault you were born that way. Didn't she say she'd be here in an hour? We need to pack, Kaali. We have some work to do."

"Am I going too?"

"Of course, you are, you fool. I don't know who else is going to fill up the van. No space? She'll probably bring that Australian paying guest she takes everywhere with her—that elephant. You can sit in the trunk. After all, I am paying two thousand rupees. What are the others paying then? Nothing, I'm sure. Always taking advantage of our bigheartedness, all of Sir's family. Nothing I ever do is enough for them."

Beneath the staircase leading to the second floor was Kaali's tiny bed, under which lay cardboard boxes that housed her prized belongings: three colorful new skirts with their price tags still on them and four hundred-rupee notes in a Liv-52 plastic container. Kaali threw the skirts into a plastic bag, forked out the notes, and shoved them in a skirt pocket. She looked at her face in her purple compact mirror, wiped the droplets of perspiration that had gathered on her forehead, and returned to help Parvati with her packing.

All you need to do is get to the Indian border, he had said. *A relative of mine will then pick you up. Here's some money for you.*

Do you know when your mistress will take you to Birtamod next? The border is just half an hour away from there.

Parvati already had a suitcase ready and was washing her hair in the kitchen sink. She ordered Kaali to hold portions of her hair while she shampooed the rest.

"Look at it falling out," Parvati said. "Soon I won't have any left."

"Your hair is thick," Kaali offered. "It will take many years for it to completely fall out."

"You know nothing. How long have you been with us? Four years? You came as a baby and still have the brains of a baby."

"I think I came when I was eight. I've been here five years."

"Yes, yes, four years, five years—what's the difference? You were nothing but bones when we brought you in. Your mother didn't want another girl child."

Parvati had narrated the story before. In fact, Kaali heard it on a weekly basis. Her mother, pressured by the growing number of mouths to feed, decided to chop off the weakest link in her family. It had to be a girl, and Kaali, with her cleft lip, was the most useless of them all. She was a sickly child, a liability who'd never be an asset. When a young widow came to their shanty in Dooars, on the India-Bhutan border, looking for a servant girl, Kaali's mother offered her for free.

"Your life was sad then," Parvati said. "Do you remember it?"

"No, I don't," Kaali replied. "I only remember my life from after I moved here."

"It's good you have no recollection. You were sick from eating all that mud outside your hut. Your brothers and sisters hated you, and I shouldn't blame them, for you were scary to look at. Your father was a useless man. I wonder if he's still alive."

"I don't remember him either."

"You don't even remember how I ran after your eight-year-old self because you had instinctively guessed I was taking you away.

What an imbecile—you had no clue you were going to lead a better life with me. You don't remember how many spoons of sugar I need. You don't even remember the insults Sarita just heaped on you. You remember nothing. What do I do with you?"

Kaali knew what was coming next. It was the underwear story. Parvati never tired of it.

"And you didn't have any underwear on, you uncivilized being—how often have I told you about the panties you wore on your head after I bought you a pair? You thought they didn't fit. Look at how far you've come, but your brains are still the same—you're still *adivasi* in your mentality."

Parvati brought up the underwear episode so frequently that Kaali no longer associated it with shame. The first few days after Kaali started living with her, Parvati made it a point to regale everyone with the story of the maid who had never before worn panties. It was on one of the various toilet breaks that punctuated their overnight bus journey from Birtamod to Kathmandu that she saw, Parvati said, to her horror, her recently acquired eight-year-old maid squat on the road, right next to the bus, and urinate, giving the world a well-defined view of her lower regions.

"And she wasn't wearing anything underneath her skirt," Parvati would say, aghast, and call for Kaali so her guests could see the little girl from the forests who had never seen panties until Parvati bought her a pair.

"Sarita told me to wipe off the snot from my face," Kaali said. "But my nose is clean, isn't it?"

You have a pretty face, he always said. *It's a pity your bad lip conceals it. Your eyes are so expressive; they are an actress's eyes. Have you ever dreamed of being an actress? Do you have a good voice? Can you sing for me?*

"You have no respect for my family members. You should call Sarita *didi*. She's my sister-in-law. Sarita is just being

condescending. She has to make others feel bad about themselves so she can feel good about herself."

"Should I pack something to eat for the road?"

"Always thinking of food, you *khanchuwee*. Must be the
extra hole in your lip that makes you hungry all the time. Yes,
pack some *chiwda* for yourself. And let me eat something here.
I'll be expected to eat some unsavory food for thirteen days. Or
maybe it's forty-five days. No salt, no oil, nothing, and I may
even be forced to eat just one meal a day. That woman is gone,
but she'll forever continue to trouble us. We have last night's
vegetables and some rice. Go warm them up for me."

As Kaali turned the gas on to warm some cauliflower, Parvati went around the house, bolting and locking the doors.

"Aye, Sarita *maiyya*, you look like you've been crying all day
long," Parvati said as she climbed into the van. "Now, you must
remember her age. She had a good life."

"No, I haven't really been crying," replied Sarita. "I didn't feel
bad, but when the servant girl told me you couldn't come to the
phone because you were crying, I felt bad that I wasn't feeling
so bad. Must have been the guilt. Aamaa never treated you well,
and yet you are sad about her death. It's funny."

Kaali, after shrugging off a stinging remark about her ugli-
ness from Sarita's teenage son, was now safely on top of all
the luggage bags in the trunk. She was staring at one of her
co-passengers—the one seated up front—and trying to hold
back a giggle. Parvati tried staring her down with bulging
eyes, but Kaali paid no attention to anyone but the old white
passenger—a big, perspiring woman who grunted when the
van finally moved.

"She didn't treat me that badly, Sarita," said Parvati. "What
family hasn't had *saasu-buhaari* spats? It's two women trying
to win the affections of the same man, so there's bound to be

some friction. You yourself told me you had problems with your mother-in-law. By the way, is this the woman staying with you?"

"Yes, although the man whose affections you were both fighting for has long been dead."

"So is your mother now. It wouldn't be right for us to talk about how she treated me. Who's this woman again?"

"Oh, this is Erin, my mother," Sarita said, and in English added, "Erin, this is my sister-in-law. I am telling her about how you're my mother from today onward."

Erin smiled at Parvati, who tried to smile back.

Sarita broke into Nepali. "She's a paying guest. She's been with me for a month. After the news of Aamaa's death today, she told me she'd be my mother from now on. I call her Aamaa, and she likes it. She wanted to see a proper Nepali funeral, so I told her to come along. You don't happen to have the money with you right now, do you? I figured we should fill up before we run out of gas in the middle of nowhere."

Be careful of the money, he reminded her every time they spoke. *Don't let anyone know you have money with you. The bus fare from Birtamod to the border should be no more than ten rupees. In fact, you may even be able to ride for free because you have the kind of pleasant disposition that inspires kindness in the most hard-hearted strangers.*

"You're taking her to attend your mother's funeral?" Parvati asked, not making an effort to hide her horror while she ferreted for two thousand-rupee notes in her purse. "Your mother dies, and you already have a new mother. That's a convenient life you lead."

"*Arrey*, you never know with these Australians. Once they like you, they could even sponsor you. In two years, you become an Australian citizen. And she's already grateful to me for taking her to my mother's—my birth mother's—funeral."

"Would it bother you if Sunny found himself another mother too?" Parvati asked, pointing at Sarita's son, who sat sulking by the window.

"Why not? If it benefits him, why not? He can even have one when I am alive."

"And when is your husband coming to the funeral?" Parvati asked.

"He may not be able to make it. He has to go to China for work tomorrow. But he'll be there for the thirteen-day *kaam*. The representatives from our family are my son, me, and Aamaa."

"Yes, your family's representatives for your dead mother's funeral are you, your son, and your new mother," Parvati said, aware the sarcasm was lost on Sarita.

They had now left the main city and the heavy traffic behind and were traversing serpentine roads. Erin clicked pictures when a particularly scenic mountain view greeted them. Sarita, ever the dutiful daughter, asked her if she wanted to get out and take photos.

"That's fine," Erin muttered.

"No, Aamaa, that's no trouble, please, please," she said and then asked the driver to stop, following which Erin got out, stared at the mountains, sighed, shot pictures, said a prayer, and got back in.

"Her camera is the size of a TV," Parvati said.

"When you use English words that way, she knows we are talking about her."

"People would think we are on a sightseeing trip and not mourning Aamaa's death," Parvati added. "And why does she keep praying? Is she calling her *Yeshu* to bless her?"

"She's a Hindu."

"Like these white people are ever Hindu."

Sarita switched to English: "Hey, Erin, my sister-in-law doesn't believe me when I tell her you're Hindu."

"Maybe I should recite the *shlokas* for her," Erin said.

"You should," Sarita replied with recently formed filial indulgence.

"So, she knows the *shlokas* too?" Parvati asked Sarita, impressed with herself for having gathered some information from a conversation in a language she barely understood.

"Yes, she does. You know, they wouldn't allow her entry into the Pashupatinath Temple; they said only Hindus allowed. She then recited the Hanuman Chalisa in front of the priests. You should have seen the look on those priests' faces."

Erin chuckled in the front seat. She turned pinker when she laughed. Kaali let out a giggle.

"Does she understand our language?" Parvati whispered.

"No, but she knows what story I am narrating because I tell it to everyone. I think it makes her proud."

"I can't believe you call her Aamaa. She doesn't even speak Nepali. I could never do it."

"But doesn't the servant girl—this one in the back—call you Aamaa?"

"No, she doesn't."

"I thought she did. Maybe you should ask her to call you Aamaa. It could make things easier for you. Does this one still steal?"

"No, Kaali doesn't steal. She's been with us five years. She's good." Parvati looked at Kaali from the corner of her eye; her servant was listening intently. "If she continues behaving, we can maybe get her lip operated on. It will cost us a lot of money, but I don't have anyone else to spend it on."

My mistress promised to get someone to teach me how to drive when I turned fifteen, he had said. *I turned sixteen, and she said I wasn't tall enough. I turned seventeen, and she said it was better to wait until the legal age. I turned eighteen, and she said I hadn't been satisfactory all of last year and didn't deserve to learn it. I didn't learn how to drive until I ran away. These people love*

*making false promises. Tell me, does your mistress tell you she will
one day get your lip fixed?*

"Yes, at least Daai built the house before he passed away.
You're lucky you don't need to save for your children's educa-
tion. Nowadays even the most stupid of them wants to go to
America. I wonder where we'll get the money from."

"We've had three deaths in six years," Parvati observed,
cautious of any money talk. "Does that say something to you?
Maybe we are cursed."

"I don't know. Baba died because he was sick and because it
was time."

"Yes, that was expected. Do you think Aamaa will go to heaven?"

"I don't think so. She has always made a lot of people suffer. She doesn't deserve to go to heaven. I know she's my
mother—my biological mother—but a fact is a fact. Thankfully,
God gave me another mother."

Sarita squeezed Erin's right shoulder and lightly massaged it.

"Don't think she only treated me badly. She was sometimes nice. Maybe if I tried to understand what she was going
through—a son's accident, a husband's passing—I'd have been
able to tolerate her better. She could have stayed with me in
Kathmandu instead of Birtamod. I could have offered."

"She'd have burned you alive if you women lived together.
She'd have sucked out your blood, minced you into pieces,
roasted you, and eaten you like a *khasi*. Honestly, Bhauju, how
did you feel when you heard the news?"

"I was sad. Ask Kaali. I couldn't help crying. I am better
now—more in control—but then the tears just wouldn't stop
flowing. They went on and on and on like the Simara rains. I
didn't know I'd be so affected by all this."

"You're definitely a better person than I'll ever be. I need to
feel sad, I know I need to cry, but I just can't. It's my mother
we're talking about, you know, my biological mother."

"Your only mother, Sarita. All this talk about another mother is nonsense."

"No, I knew you'd find the concept ridiculous. I would be grateful if you didn't. This woman is nice. You would discover how nice she is if you could talk to her."

"Oh, what will I talk to her about in my *tutey-futey* English?"

Kaali said she had to pee, which immediately flustered Sarita.

"We've only been on the road five hours, and you already have to pee?" Sarita said. "I told you to take care of your business before coming."

After they passed a resort village, from which Sarita asked the driver to stop a good distance away, because it was crowded with rafters and tourists, they all got out to stretch their legs. Sarita and Erin disappeared behind the bushes. Kaali squatted by the van, and the rivulet springing from between her legs irrigated, among other things, a colony of red ants, spurring them to zigzag their way to dryness.

"Why don't you pee standing up like a man, Kaali?" Sunny shouted from the other side of the road. "You look like a boy, and you should pee like a boy." The comment provoked a guffaw from the quiet driver.

Parvati crouched down to relieve herself where Kaali had and, spotting an ant struggle for life, asked no one in particular, "The dead, do they know when they're dying?"

"No, they don't," Kaali said with seriousness. "No, they don't know when they're dying. It just happens."

"Shut up, Kaali," Parvati said, getting in. "Talk only when you're asked something. Have you even experienced the death of a loved one to know what it feels like?"

The driver claimed the van wouldn't start because of overloading, so they all got out almost as soon as they'd got back in.

"Sunny, can you push the van?" The driver revved the engine up once again.

"Yes, Kaali should, too—she's a boy after all," Sunny yelled as he pushed the van with an exaggerated display of histrionics.

Erin joined Sunny. When the driver signaled to them that they could get in, Sarita looked proudly at Erin.

"Look, Aamaa doesn't think any job is beneath her," she said.

Within half an hour, the mauve in the sky would turn pitch black. It would be warmer as they descended into the plains, but it was getting colder now. Parvati asked Sunny to close the window on his side, but he was adamant about its remaining open. When she disagreed, they compromised that the window would be left partially open. When a truck roared past them, Parvati nudged Sarita to talk to Sunny. Sarita remained silent, forcing Parvati to take the matter up again.

"All right, Bhaanjaa, time to close the window now," she said. "We have to be well rested for the funeral, and your mother will freeze to death if you keep the window open all night."

Sunny scowled but said nothing. Sarita was quiet.

"Close the window, Bhaanjaa," Parvati said, her voice hardening slightly.

"Half an hour more, Maaiju," came the impudent reply.

"In half an hour, we'll turn into ice."

Sunny mumbled something under his breath and shut the window.

"Do you shout at him at all?" Parvati asked Sarita.

"No, not since Aamaa has lived with us. She has taught us several things about disciplining children. We allow him to do everything. She says that will make him a confident adult. She even told me not to scold him when he broke a window-pane with a cricket ball. They go on all these trips to Changunarayan and Nagarkot, and he comes back so much happier and more knowledgeable about plants and animals. I could also say he has learned more about Nepal from Aamaa than he has from us or from his exorbitant school."

"But we're different, Sarita. She's white. She's a foreigner. We bring up our children differently. We need to beat them. They need to listen to their elders. Sunny is thirteen. He'll soon be more difficult for you to manage. Thirteen to nineteen—these are crucial years."

"I don't know, Bhauju, I was beaten as a child. Aamaa —the one who died—hit me all the time. It was something I could have done without."

"But who from our generation wasn't beaten growing up? I don't know what nonsense this *gori* is feeding you, but you need to raise your children the way other Nepalis do."

At the mention of the word *gori*, Sarita quickly stole a glance at Erin, who was fast asleep. Parvati looked to see what Kaali was up to. She was spread across three big luggage bags, with a shawl covering her body from neck to toe. She gave Parvati a cheeky smile, looking more comfortable than anyone else in the van.

"I think what Aamaa says makes sense," Sarita said. "If I had been encouraged to stitch paper clothes when I was a child instead of Aamaa, the one who gave birth to me, telling me I'd end up as a low-caste tailor, I'd perhaps have been a fashion designer, making clothes for film stars. But when I said I wanted to study fashion designing, Aamaa actually had Daai give me a thrashing."

Yes, you can even become an actress once people see your real beauty after the surgery, he had said. *Bombay is a different world. I was the one who first encouraged Manisha Koirala to go to Bombay, and now look at what a big actress she has become. Of course, I can't take all the credit for it, because she was already very beautiful. You will be a film star with the nicest clothes. Now,*

*now, I must warn you not to wear those revealing clothes all these
actresses wear. That will not make me happy.*

"Daai, as in Sir?" Parvati asked, surprised that her docile
husband would be asked to carry out so brutal a task.

"Yes, your Sir," Sarita said. "He beat me with nettle leaves. He
dipped them in cold water first and then brought the *sishnu* down on
me—my hands, legs, everywhere—while Aamaa shouted encouragement. 'No one in this family becomes a *darji*,' she screamed. The
memory is still alive. I was married six months later."

"And it turned out well. You have a healthy son. Your husband makes good money. You're about to move into your own
house. I don't see how the beating did any harm."

"How do you think it looked? A grown eighteen-year-
old daughter being beaten in full view of everyone? I was so
ashamed that I refused to even walk down the street. Everyone
in the *tole* talked about it. I've never been able to forgive Daai
for it."

"You and he were never really close."

"We were, actually. It was after this episode that we drifted
apart."

"He never mentioned it to me."

"Well, you and he weren't all that close either."

"But we were married."

"That doesn't mean you share everything with each other. I
like what Aamaa says. She thinks marriages aren't so important.
The expectations are much lower when you remain unmarried."

"Your Aamaa seems like a home wrecker to me. Soon you'll
be telling me that you think divorces are acceptable."

"They should be," Sarita said. "Did I tell you I've begun going
to college?"

"*Harey*, college? At your age?"

"Yes, I joined classes at Padma Kanya three months ago.
It's strange going to class with students who are so much

younger. They are so surprised when I tell them I have a teenage son."

"They must think you're a *pagli*, Sarita. I think you are mad. You have a husband and a growing son to take care of. You need to look after them. College? At your age? Please don't tell me this was another of your Aamaa's ideas. She will soon convert you to Christianity."

"I told you she's Hindu."

"Let her be whatever she wants, but she's definitely bent on wrecking your family life. What did *jwaai* have to say?"

"He thought I was being inconsiderate, but he doesn't like to say that in front of Aamaa. When she's around, he talks about things he doesn't believe in, like women's liberation, but once she's out of the picture, he keeps telling me I am being unreasonable. He has even suggested driving her out, but because she pays so well, he can't bring himself to do it."

Suddenly their driver jerked the wheel to avoid collision as a truck from the opposite direction veered close to the van.

"*Bajiyaa*," he screamed.

The swerving and his swearing woke everyone up but Kaali.

"Drunk drivers in the night," Parvati growled.

"Is everyone okay?" Erin asked. She counted the heads and discovered the number fewer than what they had set off with. "Where's her helper?"

"She's sleeping, Aamaa," Sarita reassured her, reaching out to pat her on her shoulder. "She's fine."

"Oh, all right," Erin said, and closed her drooping eyes again.

The driver, shaken by this sudden encounter with death, asked if now might be the right time to stop for dinner. Parvati met his suggestion with happiness. She was hungry. Then, realizing that her mother-in-law's death required that she abstain from proper meals and meat for at least another thirteen days, she retreated into her shell.

"It's okay if you eat, Bhauju," Sarita said. "I couldn't eat in good conscience."

"But I was married into this family, so it's my family, Sarita. It's acceptable if you eat because you were married outside the family. Just don't eat any meat."

"She is—was—my mother. You can't possibly expect me to eat."

"But you're hungry. Maybe you could start the fasting and sacrificing tomorrow."

"Yes, why don't you, Bhauju? Tonight we eat, and tomorrow we start."

But when the driver finally pulled up to a brightly lit restaurant in a town that bustled with night buses and diners, both announced they wouldn't be able to forgive themselves if they ate. Kaali, Erin, Sunny, and the driver walked to the restaurant while Sarita and Parvati shopped for fruit and milk. They couldn't get milk thick enough for their taste anywhere this late, so they made do with tea and bananas. By the time the others had returned, Parvati and her sister-in-law had finished a dozen bananas between them. Parvati discarded her plan of surprising Kaali with a banana early in the morning as she snapped the last fruit in half.

"Six bananas each—we must have been hungry," Parvati said, hoping Sarita couldn't sleep either.

"What did you eat, Dinesh?" Sarita asked the driver.

"The food was good," Dinesh said, with an appreciative burp. "They had chicken and fish and mutton."

"Did you eat like a pig, Kaali?" Parvati asked.

"Yes, she ate quite a bit," the driver, unexpectedly talkative, answered. "But Madam ate the most. I've never seen a woman eat that way. I never knew a *kuiree* could eat so much Nepali food. Will the spices not destroy her stomach?"

Do you get to eat meat here? he had asked. *How often do you eat meat? At my mistress's place, they seldom ate meat. When they did, they usually left a smidgen of gravy and a small piece of chicken for me. I would put my plate to my face and lick it clean. Your new life will be different. You'll get to eat as much as you want, but we don't want you to be too fat. Have you seen a fat actress?*

"She's used to it. She loves Nepali food."

"Oh, she eats everything you cook?" Parvati asked, surprised.

"Yes, everything. Earlier she had a problem with the bones, but now she's used to them. She's too old to cook. Otherwise, I am sure she'd make an excellent Nepali cook."

"Maybe you could teach her. I've heard you make delicious chicken, Sarita."

"I am learning other recipes. I am taking a home science class at PK. We get to experiment a lot."

"So, you're actually going to college to do a course you could study at home?" Parvati asked.

"No, this is just one of the classes. I've many others. I like this one best. Maybe I could do a bachelor's in home science, then a master's."

"Who's heard of a mother of a teenage son with such ambitions? I think you're throwing a lot of time and money down the drain."

"No, I am not. As Aamaa says, this is an investment. Education is always an investment."

"Now you're talking like Kaali. She's been asking to be sent to school for some time now."

"Why don't you? She doesn't do a lot during the day."

"What will she do with an education and that face? It will all be a wasted effort."

"She wouldn't bother you during the day," Sarita countered.

"I want her home during the day."

"She keeps you company, doesn't she? I always knew you were very attached to her."

"Who gets attached to a servant, Sarita? But, yes, she keeps me company. If I had a son—or even a daughter—to keep me busy, like you do, I'd happily accept it and live that life. If I had a living husband, like you do, I'd attend to his needs and concentrate on making him happy instead of running off to some college."

"I know, Bhauju, you wouldn't expect to hear this from anyone, but I like your life." Sarita looked straight ahead. "I envy the life you live."

"Why would anyone envy a widow's life, Sarita?" Parvati let out a sigh. "I have nothing to look forward to—no school, no children whose marriages to await, no sons to look after me, no husband's arrival at home to anticipate, no daughter's well-being to be afraid for—and I must be among the most miserable women there are. I wouldn't wish my life on my enemy, Sarita."

"See, that's why. The only bad thing about your life was the occasional visit from your mother-in-law, who's now dead. You don't have a husband who questions your decisions. You don't have a child who frustrates you with his mischief. You don't have to save for his future. If I were you, I'd use Daai's pension money on pilgrimages to Benares, Bodh Gaya, Tirupathi, everywhere in India. You can pack your bags and leave for anywhere any day. You have no children's vacation days to coordinate and no household budget holding you back."

"I am still a widow, Sarita," Parvati said. "I am a Nepali widow. I get discriminated against. You'll see that when we reach Birtamod I won't be allowed to take part in any of the rituals. The world looks at us widows differently. When we haven't been able to give birth, the stigma we face only becomes worse. I look at the colorful *potey* you wear around your neck and the thickness of your *sindoor*, and I get jealous. I have even stopped celebrating *Teez*. Why would I do that? I am a widow, you see."

*   *   *

The driver stopped the van and got out to relieve himself. It was obvious, however, that he didn't want to smoke in their presence.

"Let him smoke," Parvati said. "He has to stay awake. He doesn't need to hide from us. What a respectful young man."

Sarita checked if Sunny was asleep and then asked, "Have you ever smoked, Bhauju?"

"Why would I?"

"Never at all?"

"I tried *khaini* once, but it put my entire mouth on fire. Never trying it again. I am not going to ask you if you've tried smoking, but I have a feeling you have."

"Yes, I have."

"When?"

"Some girls in college decided to try some *Hulas* after school. I took several puffs, too. It relaxed me."

"Something tells me that wasn't the only time."

"No, I smoke about one every day before I head home. It helps me think with a clear head. Only Aamaa knows about it. She doesn't approve of doing it around Sunny."

When she saw the driver return, Sarita pinched Parvati, signaling that they should stop talking about the matter.

"Well, at least I am glad it's not the *gori* who has yet again put another idea into your head," Parvati said.

"Aamaa has been a calming influence in my life. She'd never condone that."

They had barely covered a few kilometers when, a few minutes before they would have reached the Koshi Barrage, a flat tire befell them.

"Every time I have traveled this road, I have fallen prey to a puncture," Parvati said. "It's like the road has nails and needles growing on it."

"Thankfully, the Maoists do tourists no harm, so once they see Aamaa with us, we are safe," Sarita said with a yawn. "Aamaa is so important."

The Maoists have destroyed Nepal, he had said. *Even if you escape the clutches of your cruel mistress one day, what will you do in this country? Join the Maoists? Carry a gun and shoot innocent villagers? Give in to their extortions? It's time for you to leave the country and make a life for yourself, Kaali. The rich go to America, to England. You will go to Bombay and become the biggest star in Bollywood.*

"Come here," Parvati said to Kaali, who, after getting out from the back of the van, seemed lost. "You'll be safe here."

Kaali hesitantly moved in her direction.

"It looks like you were the most comfortable of us all. Are you hungry? Go eat some *chiwda.*"

"I couldn't sleep at all. I heard you talk about me."

"Liar. You were almost snoring when we stopped for dinner."

Kaali's loud chewing of beaten rice complemented the clanging of the driver's tools. Erin and Sarita had vanished into the jungle despite Parvati's warning them not to wander off too far. When they returned, Sarita looked fresher than before. Parvati guessed that her sister-in-law had smoked a cigarette. The gum Sarita was chewing could hardly disguise the smell.

Once the tire was replaced and all returned to their seats, the driver complained to Sarita about tiredness. A little music would keep him awake for the remainder of the drive, but the van had no radio, he said. Sarita repeated his predicament to Erin, who handed him her Discman and showed him how to wear the headphones before falling back asleep. Parvati and Sarita smiled in the backseat.

Some silence later, Sarita said, "I am thinking of divorcing him."

Parvati let out a yelp. All along, she had sensed the warm-up conversation was leading somewhere—maybe her sister-in-law would talk about some murky waters she was in with her husband's family or financial troubles she'd need Parvati's help to get out of—but Parvati wasn't expecting news of this magnitude. Divorce? Divorce was something that didn't happen in their world. You heard about a woman filing for divorce when the beatings from her husband got unbearable. You talked about how ostracized a woman became after the divorce. You talked about some rich hotelier's wife wanting a divorce. What made the idea of divorce even more inappropriate was that Sarita was talking about it not twenty-four hours after her mother's death.

"You haven't slept," Parvati said. "And you're talking nonsense because you're in shock about your mother's death. You need sleep."

"No, I am serious. I feel alive. I feel right. And I am glad I am talking about it with you. Daai is dead, and he was our only connection. I've nothing to gain and nothing to lose from you. We barely see each other once a year. You are the right person to talk to."

"I am still your dead brother's wife, Sarita," Parvati feebly said, all the while fully registering that Sarita was right. The one bond between them—her husband, Sarita's brother—was long gone. They didn't know each other very well. In fact, Parvati didn't even remember what Sarita's *dera* in Teenkune looked like—that's how long ago she had last been there despite the close distance—and she didn't know Sarita's phone number. They were practically strangers, so the fear of being judged wasn't so severe. It was natural for her sister-in-law to confide in her. That she chose a few hours before her mother's funeral to do so was only circumstantial. If this was the only time in the last year they had seen each other, there was no better—or worse—time to share.

"Aamaa thinks I have the ability to do a lot more in the world," Sarita said.

"The world is your family, Sarita. What you do with them is how you use your potential."

"I know you think Aamaa is useless, but she's the first person who has shown an appreciation for my opinions and talents. She has encouraged me to take up sewing again. I gathered the courage to go to college because of her. If she wants to help me realize my dreams, why should I stop her?"

You need to be someplace you will be appreciated, not shouted at all day long, he had said. *I am not going to lie—the process of becoming a famous star will be difficult. You will have to forget a great deal of what you've been taught. The competition is tough, and my cousin will teach you about things you might have to do with rich, powerful men to gain favor from them. You've a bright future, Kaali, don't let your mistress tell you otherwise. You have to promise not to forget about us lesser people when you are rich. All right, promise me that, keti.*

"And what about your husband and son, Sarita? They should be your dream. This college dream will end once you realize how difficult life is alone. I've done it, and it isn't nice. At least you have a husband who doesn't beat you up. You've been married fourteen years. Don't throw it all away on this wild notion of love. We are Nepalis. We are different from these people."

"But I've been unhappy, Bhauju, really, really unhappy. I love my son and thought I'd suffer through this for him, but—"

"What sufferings are you talking about, Sarita? Suffering is your husband beating you up, coming home drunk, and throwing utensils at your head. Suffering is your husband cavorting with other women and having mistresses. Suffering is not having a husband at all. You have a husband, and he is a nice, reliable man. He takes care of your son and is a good father. He has even allowed you to go to college although he clearly doesn't like it. Why throw it all away just because some white woman lectures you on love? She sees marriage through her Western eyeglasses. What you and *jwaai* have is special. Don't let anyone—least of all a sixty-year-old white woman who's spent her life alone and is now living in a foreign country with a foreign family—tell you otherwise. It's a great marriage. You just need to be on the outside to see how beautiful it is."

"Aamaa says I could go to Australia."

"You could also go to Australia with your husband and son. You could start a new life there with your husband and son. You could work, study, earn with your husband and son by your side. You don't need to sacrifice one to have the other. You'll have disagreements, arguments, and fights, but that's the beauty in it. If I could bring your brother back from the dead, even if I were told all we'd do once he came back is fight, I'd happily have him. Life is so much better when you have someone to share it with. You don't want to be alone, Sarita. Five years of loneliness has half killed me. I sometimes don't recognize who I am. I see fully the differences between the person I was before your brother passed away and the person I am now. Take my advice—talk it out with your husband. He might be willing to move to Australia. If it's a great opportunity, why not? Then talk to your Aamaa. Tell her you can't leave your husband because you don't want to. If she's the goddess you claim she is, I am sure she'll understand."

The sun grew stronger as a new day stretched ahead and the van stuffier with the progression of the journey. Sunny awoke and right away opened his window, letting a breeze blow in. Erin asked for her Discman back, opened her window, and took pictures. The driver was mellow, his near-death experience several hours earlier discouraging him from overtaking larger vehicles.

When Kaali tried sitting up, the van abruptly made a turn, and she hit her head on the roof.

"That was just stupid Kaali," Sarita said to her husband on the phone. "Can't even stand straight. All right, I have to go now. We are almost here. Can you hear the conches? Looks like they've already donated a cow—wait, it's a calf—to the priest. Bye. Be careful of what you eat in that strange land—don't they eat anything that has four legs? *Chyaaa.*"

"Kaali is such a bad name, Kaali," Parvati said. "From now on, introduce yourself to everyone as Rekha."

"Rekha is a good name." Sarita giggled. "Rekha, like the actress."

Kaali looked bewildered.

"And maybe, Sarita, while we are in Birtamod, after the thirteen-day ceremony is over, we could go to Siliguri."

You will stay in Siliguri for a few days before going to Bombay, he had said. *You have to do as my cousin says. He's a nice person but can lose his temper easily. Remember he has nothing to gain out of you—he's doing you a favor because I have convinced him of your potential. You have to understand that everything he makes you do, even if you've been taught that it is wrong, is a stepping-stone to your becoming a big star.*

"I hear these cleft-lip surgeries are a lot cheaper in India than in Kathmandu," Parvati said as she headed to the house, and added in a whisper, "I am too tired to make arrangements for a separate room for me to mourn in. I hope they've already taken care of that."

"I'll help you, Bhauju," Sarita offered.

"Kaali, Kaali," Parvati shouted. "Yes, stare longingly at the road, like the overnight journey wasn't enough. Or do you want to go home to your poor family? You know that's the way to them."

"Oh, so this is the way to India?" Kaali asked.

"Yes, fool, it is."

Kaali was quiet for a while. "I have four hundred rupees I brought with me," she said. "It might get lost in the *halla-gulla* here, so will you please keep it?"

"Where did you get the money from? Have you been stealing?"

"No, no, this is the money I earned from my singing during *Tihaar*."

"Yes, must be. I keep forgetting you went singing with that terrible voice of yours from house to house. Maybe people didn't throw you out because they were feeling bighearted during the festival season. Shouldn't you have given it to me before we set off, Kaali? Give it to me, okay, but don't make a scene out of it. Time and place for everything, girl, time and place for everything."

LET SLEEPING DOGS LIE

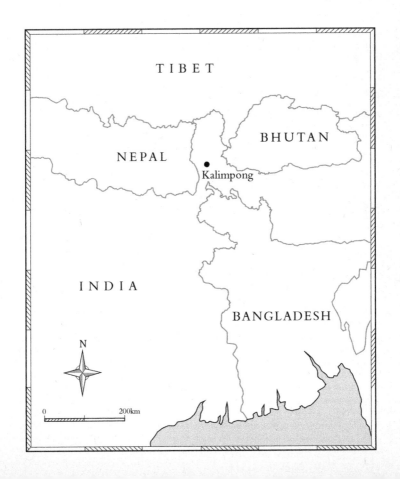

Munnu—no one knew if that was his real name—momentarily stopped ruminating about his troublesome wife to return the greeting of the gigantic girl in front of him and smiled. Yet the smile did not stretch to his eyes—the eyes looked shiftily at her, nervous and uncomfortable.

"Are you all right, Bahini?" Munnu asked, his lips still a smile, his stare faltering. "Have you eaten lunch yet?"

"No, Aamaa isn't home, and the servant is sick," Shraddanjali replied. "I might need some noodles. I am hungrier than these coolies' kids."

She was polite, exaggeratedly so. She made it a point to wish Namaste not just to her neighbors and friends' parents but also to the servants. The flustered servants, unused to this display of respect from the child of a rich man, grinned back and sometimes hurriedly broke into a Namaste before she did. This kind of niceness coming from the daughter of someone so important was embarrassing, and while some initially decided that she was mocking them—theirs is after all a class that everyone disrespects, even the drivers, and is accustomed to being ridiculed—they came around to accepting her frequent greetings with the obsequiousness ingrained in their psyche.

Munnu knew she would ask for noodles. Shraddanjali was also talking more than she should. She often did that, and he was aware of what it resulted in.

"Wai Wai or Maggi, Bahini?" he asked.

"Let me take one Wai Wai and one Maggi. Both vegetarian."

Munnu Bhaiya turned to the section housing noodles and chips on shelves that reached all the way to the ceiling of his L-shaped store. For their everyday needs, the neighborhood people—and pedestrians who passed by the busy thoroughfare leading to the bus stand—depended on Munnu's convenience store for *paan*, chips, chocolate bars, toffees, condoms (safely concealed in a drawer, of course), soft drinks, pens, notebooks, and cigarettes.

His landlords, the famous doctor-architect couple of Kalimpong, had begrudgingly rented out a little space on the road-level floor to Munnu at minimal cost. The husband had grunted that a *paan* store would not play well with the aesthetics of their seven-story building—a beautiful construction painstakingly built with more money than they'd spent on any single thing besides their only daughter's unsuccessful leukemia treatment—but Munnu had been persistent. He promised to keep the store free of flies and offered to clean not just the storefront but also the stairs. The landlords liked Munnu. He was less businessman-like than his father—the scumbag who was rumored to soon be taking up residence in Mecca, of all places—and they patronized Munnu's store as much as they could.

With Munnu renting the space, a hundred-square-foot area lay empty. A travel agency, advertising trips to the few tourist spots in town with red, green, and yellow lettering stenciled on the door, was paying good money for the rest of the floor. Neither Munnu nor the travel agency owner wanted the spare room. The landlords had tried using it as a garage for their little Hyundai Santro, but the first night their chauffeur drove in, the building vibrated with an intensity they hadn't felt since their dead daughter skipped over her new rope on the terrace. The garage stood empty for the better part of the year until another *Musalmaan* asked to rent it out. He would match what Munnu was paying. So it happened that two *paan* stores, side by side, one tinier than another but both very small, stood on the road level.

Initially, Munnu had been nervous about a competitor next door selling exactly the same goods his shop stocked, but he soon realized his fears were unfounded. All of this part of Relli Road, the neighborhood in the vicinity of Baidyanath, came to him as creatures of habit. Sure, to passersby, the two stores were the same, and Munnu found the foot traffic decrease slightly soon after, but that wasn't anything to be overly concerned about. Should the new shop eat into substantial profits, he'd simply talk to the landlords about renting the formerly vacant space. In fact, as a precautionary measure, he'd ask them to rent him the place before the other store's lease was up. What paltry business his store lost now was hardly cause for an anxiety attack. What was worth one throbbing headache was this animal in front of him.

At almost six feet tall, she was maybe the tallest girl in Kalimpong. Hers was one of those faces you couldn't do so much about, which Munnu thought was a pity, because each one of her features, isolated from the rest, was rather striking. The combination resulted in an unremarkable face—not downright ugly but slightly incongruous. Munnu, who prided himself in his ability to determine what was amiss in a woman's attractiveness, knew she'd have been far better looking if some part of her face were slightly ugly—maybe a bucktooth here or a bump on the nose there. It was evident she tried too hard. She was a high school girl, but she wore thick, luminous lip gloss that rivaled the shine of her artificially colored burgundy hair.

He had seen this girl grow. She frequently beat up neighborhood boys as a grisly overweight child, but she was now as thin as a bamboo stick. On days she was sick and absented herself from school, she'd puff into his store, dressed in just a shawl and pajamas with pictures of red hearts on them, asking for a pack of Good Day or Bourbon biscuits. "The Well-Mannered Terror" his father and he had nicknamed her. Munnu was still a little afraid of her. She has a mole on her upper lip, he reasoned, which means she will always have a sharp tongue. Always a sharp tongue, he thought with a gentle shudder.

"I don't see your daughter anymore," said Shraddanjali to his back as she opened the glass-topped rectangular box on the counter. In it were rows of chocolate bars—foreign imports along with Dairy Milk and Fruit & Nut—more expensive than the ones consigned to jars.

Munnu heard a thud and a clink behind him but didn't turn. He'd have to find a way to move the stack of noodles near his seat at the counter. He continued chewing the last remains of his *zardaa paan*, which he had recently developed a preference for over the more innocent *meetha* one, and wrapped the Wai Wai and Maggi with page three of a three-week-old newspaper. Having finished his job, he let his eyes wander to the green lipstick a Bollywood actress wore, coughed three times, and, still with his back to Shraddanjali, asked her if she wanted anything else.

"I hope you have a plastic bag today," Shraddanjali said.

"No." Munnu turned around. "Environment. Remember?"

"*Oooof*, your concern for the environment has inconvenienced us. At least you should supply us with paper bags before you do away with all plastic."

"Right, Bahini, right, other customers, too, keep complaining. Leezum's mother has even threatened to go to the Munnu next door to do her shopping if I don't keep a hidden supply of plastic bags. But what can I do? I promised myself and those students from Dr. Graham's Homes."

His reference to the other store owner as "Munnu" delighted Shraddanjali.

"You call him Munnu, too?" She laughed, gathering her package. "We call him Chunnu. What's his real name anyway?"

Munnu didn't know his neighbor's name either.

"Munnu Two," he said.

They laughed the laugh of two people who had known each other a long time but were still uncomfortable with the vast gulf separating one's silver-spoon upbringing from another's fast-improving but modest existence.

"Okay, I need to go boil these now," Shraddanjali said. "I hate it when I have to work."

Munnu was certain that Shraddanjali would whine some more, as she always did when she took from the store more than what she paid for. But when Dr. Pradhan, the building's owner, appeared, Shraddanjali stopped talking.

"Shraddanjali, my *naani*, not so little anymore, huh?" Dr. Pradhan said as the teenager joined her hands in Namaste to her. "Ah, now you will stop growing, and now you can buy all these pretty clothes when you go to Delhi University. How excited you must be."

"Yes, Auntie, very excited, but I still have my exams to study for before that," Shraddanjali said. "And what if I don't get into Delhi University?"

"You will, don't worry," Mrs. Pradhan said. "How's your mother doing?"

"She's fine, Auntie, very fine. But I have to leave now. The servant is out, and Aamaa isn't even home."

Shraddanjali again joined her hands in Namaste. Not many young people did that when taking leave.

"How big she's grown, Munnu Bhaiya," Dr. Pradhan said, and after confirming Shraddanjali was out of earshot, mumbled, "Very well-ironed skirt or belt. Or whatever."

"She looks well mannered, but she isn't, Memsaab," Munnu complained.

"Has she been doing it again?" Dr. Pradhan asked.

"Every day she comes here—sometimes one chocolate, sometimes two. Today it was two."

"Soon you'll be operating at a loss, Munnu Bhaiya."

"But what can I do, Memsaab? She's a big person's daughter. I can't accuse her of anything."

"Hire a helper, Munnu."

"I can't afford one, Memsaab," Munnu said.

"Maybe you could just talk to the parents."

"Yes, but she's eighteen. Talking to the parents about an eight-year-old's bad habits is reasonable, but this is a full-grown *haathi* we are talking about."

"Don't speak about my friend's daughter that way, Munnu Bhaiya," Mrs. Pradhan said.

"See, that's my point, Memsaab," Munnu replied, unable to make out the seriousness of his landlady's admonishment. "If I tell someone else about it, who will believe me? I am a Bihari *Musalmaan paanwalla*, and she's the daughter of the biggest lawyer in Kalimpong."

"It's a disease—I forget what they call it in English," said Dr. Pradhan. "How are your wife and daughter? I'll see them in a little while now."

Munnu was born in Kalimpong. He was brought up—motherless—in Kalimpong. His father, successful to the extent that a *paan*-shop owner could be, dragged his toddler to the store under the excuse that Munnu would have had no one to look after him at home. Munnu had grown up in his father's store. Neighbors and customers often asked the senior *paan-walla* why he didn't provide his son a formal education, to which the gruff man replied that there was no better school than the shop. And he might have been right. Munnu recognized his first letter at the store; he learned to add at the store. He also discovered how to make people like him (his father wasn't a popular man, and his ruthlessness as a part-time moneylender was well known) with his ready smile, inquiries into their lives, and a compassionate ear.

Munnu didn't let the truth of his family's being wealthier than most of his middle-class customers get to his head. Despite knowing no home other than Kalimpong, he knew he would never totally belong here, that he'd always be considered an outsider, and listening to his customers' problems without asserting his superiority would be the easiest way for him to be one of them—or come close to being one of them. He was so much of a Kalimpong man that he thought in Nepali and not in Bhojpuri or Urdu. Despite all that, assimilation had its limitations, and Munnu didn't mind that. He was, after all, living in a region that was vocal—and sometimes violent—in its demand for a separate state based on ethnic differences, so it was normal for ethnic affinities to compound.

Only two years ago, after helping Munnu set up shop and leasing his own store to another Muslim businessman, his father took up the task of finding a bride for his son. The old man's attempts at finding a decent girl in Kalimpong were futile. First, the number of Muslims in town was negligible. And second, the girls were either educated—an idea both Munnu and his father were wary of—or belonged to poor families, which meant a measly dowry.

Soon, father and son expanded their search to include Darjeeling, Siliguri, and Kurseong. Finding no one suitable even there, they stretched their territories farther and settled on a fifth cousin from Meerut, far away in Uttar Pradesh. Munnu would have preferred someone who spoke Nepali, but he had long ago reconciled himself to his narrow options. And Humera was really fair—white like the best-quality flour he sold. A color TV and furnishings came in the dowry.

Humera stood out in Kalimpong for one big reason. The color of her skin played no role in her attracting the town's attention. In fact, her looks had nothing to do with it—it was what covered her fair face that piqued everyone's interest. She was the only woman in the entire town to don a burqa. In Kalimpong, a few Muslim women veiled their faces, as did some Marwari wives, but no one wore a burqa. No amount of coercing on Munnu's part persuaded his otherwise subservient wife to give up her favorite accessory. Munnu would have been happy if his wife had veiled herself, but a burqa—anachronistic and out of place—was taking it too far. He was afraid that everyone in town would assume that he made his wife wear it.

Humera had just given him a daughter, which had disturbed his father and resulted in the trip to Mecca. Munnu would have preferred a son, but he wasn't unhappy with the girl. He planned on sending her to school, at least up to Class Three. He had grown to like his wife, although many aspects of her personality baffled him. She was horrified when he cooed to the baby using Nepali words. She was unyielding about the burqa. She repeatedly reminded him when he forgot to offer *Namaaz*. She sometimes apologized for having given birth to a daughter. Besides these few quirks, she was everything Munnu had wanted in a wife—she was fair and beautiful (not that he could show that off), submitted to his needs (not that he demanded anything unreasonable), and cooked very well (not that he was a glutton). She also disliked traveling, so there had been no visits to her parents' place since the marriage, which Munnu couldn't complain about.

Humera's mother was too sick to travel to Kalimpong, so when Munnu disclosed to Dr. Pradhan that his wife was pregnant, the landlady played surrogate.

"She hasn't seen a doctor since she fell pregnant?" Dr. Pradhan had shouted at Munnu. "What age are you Muslims living in?"

"She doesn't like seeing doctors."

"Who does? It's going to a doctor, not a *Dashain* celebration, not an *Eid* celebration."

"She doesn't like *Eid* celebrations either."

"Now is not the time to joke, Munnu. Tomorrow, after my shift at the hospital, I shall come see her. Please see to it that your apartment is clean for that."

"I don't know if she'd be willing." Munnu gave her an apologetic look.

"Then have a deformed baby and be happy with it," Dr. Pradhan said with uncharacteristic anger.

At home, he asked Humera to be prepared for a visit. He had never seen her so livid.

"Think of it," he reasoned. "If she's not happy with me, she could throw us out of her building. What will the baby eat if we have no shop? She has lost her own child, so she just wants to make sure ours is okay."

Humera had finally relented, but only on the condition that the landlady be allowed just one visit. Dr. Pradhan criticized Munnu for considering a midwife. When Munnu remarked it wasn't his idea but his wife's and that he'd definitely be more comfortable with a doctor involved, Dr. Pradhan scolded Humera. One visit turned to two, three, and four. How someone in his landlady's position mingled so freely with an illiterate, orthodox Muslim like his wife confused Munnu. Maybe it had something to do with the loss of her daughter; perhaps she had found an excellent listener in Humera. Initially, he was happy about it.

Then things began to change. Little by little, his wife started talking back to him. Again, he was pleasantly surprised that she had grown a spine, but when the retorts became snarkier and more common, he knew he'd have to put a stop to it. He threatened to beat her if she continued misbehaving. Humera retaliated that she'd tell Dr. Pradhan about it, which would jeopardize his relationship with the landlords.

Humera had now been talking about making her own money by helping in Dr. Pradhan's pediatric clinic. It would be only babies and women, she argued. That, he wasn't going to allow. Thankfully, she still wore her burqa. He regretted ever having pestered her to give it up for a veil.

Dr. Pradhan was close to both Munnu and his wife, but she never saw them together. She only interacted with Munnu at the store, and she and Humera visited at home. With Humera, Munnu wondered if she discussed how to be a modern woman. With Munnu, she discussed business and the store. And Shraddanjali.

Six months ago, when both Shraddanjali and she were at the store, Dr. Pradhan noticed her pilfer a cigarette from behind the counter. Shraddanjali must have thought she was being cautious, but the landlady was wearing her sunglasses, a pair too large for her face, and that made it difficult to tell exactly where she was looking. The moment Shraddanjali left, Dr. Pradhan's eyes met Munnu's, and Munnu Bhaiya, her tenant, broke down and told her everything.

It had gone on for ten years, even when he ran his father's store, he said. When she was a child, she stole the occasional cheap toffee. Sometimes, she bought two toffees for a rupee and returned minutes later to exchange one for a different type. She'd then open the bottle in which the candy belonged, throw it in and fish a different sweet from another jar. Munnu soon discovered—when a taxi-stand regular broke his tooth on it—that the returned toffee was actually a pebble in a sweet wrapper. In the beginning, Munnu had found the petty stealing endearing.

But the thefts increased in frequency and intensity over time. Shraddanjali no longer stole fifty-paise toffees these days but went after cigarettes—entire packs of them—or chocolate bars, the expensive ones that cost more than twenty rupees. And it happened almost every time she came to the store, which was almost every day.

Dr. Pradhan had listened with exaggerated clucking and concern. Since then, Munnu shared everything about Shraddanjali's thefts with her. Theirs was a special bond, a relationship that had grown with Shraddanjali's escalating bravado—Munnu went over what Shraddanjali had stolen that day or the day before, and Dr. Pradhan would estimate the losses he incurred. On a particularly expensive day, Dr. Pradhan insisted that Munnu talk to Shraddanjali's parents, but the *paanwalla* was unconvinced it would do him any good.

"I am a *Musalmaan* who enjoys a very good place here," he repeatedly reasoned. "I make more money than any other storekeeper, and everyone trusts me. I wouldn't think of doing anything that might disrupt that. Let sleeping dogs lie."

"Soon, she'll be stealing these scents here." Dr. Pradhan pointed at the little unlocked shelf of mysteriously spelled Calvin Klein and Dolce & Gabbana cologne bottles, all neatly set with more reverence than they received at the cosmetic stores on Main Road.

Soon enough, that's what happened. Every time her friend had a birthday, Shraddanjali was at the store, greeting Munnu with a Namaste and asking for packs of Maggi before she opened the sliding glass door and pretended to peruse the new arrivals while still making small talk. All she had to do, after this, was to deposit the cologne bottles in her purse—she had begun carrying a purse—while Munnu reached out for her noodles.

Munnu didn't keep an inventory of everything in the store, but he knew how many cologne bottles there were. The margin of profit might be the highest in colognes, but they also cost a lot

to begin with. Twenty bottles would trickle down to nineteen—
sometimes eighteen—with Shraddanjali's departure. This was
costlier than five chocolate bars put together. The profits were
getting scantier every month.

"Today there were three bottles of scent gone," he said to
Dr. Pradhan one evening.

"Yes, it's her mother's birthday tomorrow," Dr. Pradhan
remarked. "I assume that will be the gift."

"Oh, you all celebrate birthdays at this age, Memsaab?"

"At this age? What do you mean, *Paanwalla*? Of course, we
don't. We just get together for lunch or something."

"But that is celebrating, right?" He laughed.

"Maybe you should have a big birthday for your daughter
when she turns one soon."

"We are Muslims, you see. We don't celebrate girls' birthdays."

"You live in Kalimpong now, Munnu, you need to adapt to
the ways here. Forget Bihar, forget Islam."

"I wonder if I should talk to her mother now." Munnu had
become adept at changing the course of a conversation. "It's just
gone on for too long."

"I'd do that. I'd really do that if I were you."

"You know I can't, Memsaab, you know how it is. Her father
is powerful. What if he puts me in jail?"

"I would like it if you came to me if my daughter were stealing." His landlady was stoic.

"It's risky."

"If you can't, then don't complain, *Paanwalla*. As it is,
you're making *lakhs*. Hire a runner—a starving boy from your
hometown."

"No, Memsaab, the storekeeper next door is stealing a lot of
my customers. I want to talk to you and Saab about taking his
space, too. The profits aren't what they used to be. That's why I
can't hire anyone."

"Don't complain to me. Saab likes that two stores complete the look of the building. He thinks they make for a twisted visual harmony—if only I knew what that means. You don't have cards here, do you? Birthday cards, anniversary cards? Maybe I will buy Mrs. Gurung a card for her birthday. It'll be a nice gesture."

"For the mother of a thief, yes, a very nice gesture," said Munnu bitterly.

"Don't speak that way, Munnu, don't forget they are rich, powerful people. Just because I talk to you like you're not a *paanwalla*, like you're one of us, doesn't mean you can talk ill of my friends. Try to stay in your place. I'd talk politely to her parents. I admit no one wants to know her daughter is a thief, but you need to stay afloat. And poor Mrs. Gurung, I wonder how many people you share her daughter's stories with. I am sure I am not the only one."

"No, Memsaab, you're the only one," Munnu said. "No one really knows about it."

"Oh, then, boy, do I feel special, a *paanwalla* reveals the secrets of his trade to me."

She laughed a high-pitched laughter, spiteful and loud, so passersby looked at her and their eyes locked in unison against the stupidity of this *Musalmaan*, this *paanwalla*.

"Sorry, Memsaab, if I offended you," Munnu said. "It's just that you talk so nicely to us small people that I feel I can share anything with you, even if it involves your friend's daughter."

"Don't worry about it, Munnu." Dr. Pradhan was placated. "Maybe I will give Mrs. Gurung a hint tomorrow. She won't be thrilled, but we can't have this continue. I'll let her know I saw it happen and that you said nothing to me."

That was a very generous offer. But generosity came easily to Dr. Pradhan. She had, after all, taken upon herself to make his wife a woman of the times. Humera had still not stopped her nonsense about working.

* * *

Munnu was changing stations on his radio and scratching his lower abdomen, his hands moving surreptitiously toward his crotch, when a hassled Mrs. Gurung charged at the store.

"You called my daughter a thief, you *kukkur*." Mrs. Gurung almost leapt at him. "You'll see what happens when you do that."

Mrs. Gurung was still in her floral nightgown. No one ever saw her in a nightgown beyond her verandah.

Munnu Bhaiya was nervous. He tried to smile, but because he was in the midst of chewing *paan*, the open mouth—a mixture of green, red, and saffron—gave an entirely different effect.

"Spit that *paan* out, you *Musalmaan*," the woman screamed, a sprinkling of saliva landing on the glass-topped rectangular box her daughter had stolen thousands of rupees' worth of chocolate bars from.

Because Munnu always swallowed the remains of his *paan*, he didn't have a trash can around. Without a moment's thought, he spat out the *paan* remains into his palm.

"Look at that, you brainless *baandar*, look at what you do. You people don't bathe, don't wash your hands after shitting, and now you spit your *paan* into your hands. And you then call my daughter a thief? What has my daughter stolen from you?"

By now a crowd had gathered outside. Most were laborers from the nearby taxi stand. They spent their slow days playing cards, chewing tobacco, and smoking *beedis*. They also scuttled in packs to where they could find commotion.

"*Oye*, the *Musalmaan*, the nicer one, is in trouble," someone said. "He called that lawyer Memsaab's daughter a whore."

"Isn't she one?" another quipped on the scramble there.

"And now all the coolies are here," Mrs. Gurung barked. "Don't you have any work to do, you idiots? You're also as disrespectful as this *paanwalla* here. At least as Nepali people, you should help a Gurkha sister. Why does no one beat this dog up? I challenge someone to. A *Musalmaan* insults Kalimpong's own daughter, and all you Nepalis do is stand and watch the *tamasha*. All of you Nepali coolies should be sent back to Nepal if you can't defend one Nepali's honor when a Bihari insults her daughter."

Mrs. Gurung was hissing now. The prospect of being beaten up enraged Munnu at first and shortly after made him cry.

"Now cry, you eunuch, you donkey," Mrs. Gurung continued her tirade, punctuating it with a slap. "This will teach you not to talk about bigger people, you fool."

Pulling her shawl closer together to cover up her nightgown, she stormed out.

Ashamed and fearful, Munnu shut up shop early and narrated the episode to Humera. He eliminated the portion where he was slapped—it was too emasculating—but she'd hear it from someone sooner or later, most definitely from Dr. Pradhan.

"I am afraid that other customers will think I am spreading rumors about them," he said as he retired for the night. That would eventually result in losing more customers to the new store—a nightmare.

He couldn't sleep. He wished his daughter would cry to keep his mind off the day he had just had. He switched on his color TV and changed channels aimlessly with the remote.

When his wife finally awoke in the morning, she told him that because he didn't permit her to take up Dr. Pradhan's job offer, somebody else would be hired. She said she'd likely ask around for jobs—any job—all day.

"Any job?" he asked.

She nodded.

Munnu had an epiphany.

Excited, he dressed and ran the flight of stairs to Mrs. Gurung's house. He apologized to both Mr. and Mrs. Gurung and added that it was probably his wife who had been stealing.

"Don't blame your wife," Mrs. Gurung, far removed from the woman she was yesterday, consoled. "It wouldn't be stealing if it is her husband's store."

"I didn't talk to anyone about it, just to Dr. Pradhan." Munnu was speaking the truth.

"She's a gossipy woman, Munnu," Mrs. Gurung said. "After her daughter's death, she's been looking for some purpose in life. She loves drama. That's perhaps why I reacted so badly."

"I hope Shraddanjali doesn't know I falsely blamed her."

"No, she does not, Munnu."

With a spring in his step, he rushed to the store.

The next day, Shraddanjali appeared at the shop with a bear—the smallest bear, the kind young women these days attached to their T-shirt sleeves.

"Isn't it your daughter's birthday?" she asked Munnu while joining her hands together for him. "I've brought this *Chui-mui* for her."

"Hello, Bahini, it is a week from today," he said.

"I have a little present for her. Where is she? Oh, and why don't I take a Wai Wai and a Maggi? You know the servant's not home again. And could you pack them up, too? Everyone thinks I've been eating so much. I don't want them to talk too much about me."

She was rambling. He knew what that meant, but he was prepared today.

"You didn't have to buy a birthday gift for Albeli." He smiled.

His smile extended all the way to his eyes, forming tiny creases. There was a very slight twinkle, too.

His wife would arrive at the store any moment now for her second day of training. She had mastered the calculator pretty fast for someone who had never used one. With the two of them in the store, he didn't have to work as hard as before, and the counter was never unmanned. He had made one last effort to convince Humera to abandon the burqa, but she wasn't going to lose it. That didn't mean she wouldn't be able to see through it.

A Father's Journey

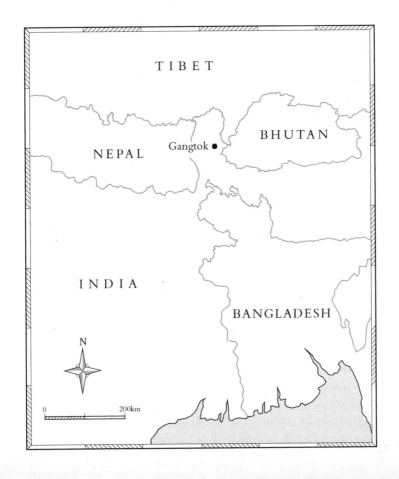

Notebook in hand, Supriya lazily stretched her tiny legs across the sofa and onto her father's lap, struggling to align the slash of her Nepali words with the lines on the paper. She ignored the blare of the TV and the sound of her mother's knife rapping the cutting board. Occasionally, she'd stop tapping her feet and glance at the screen to ask her father, Prabin, if what he was watching was funny or sad, brushing off her mother's reprimand not to get distracted.

After dinner, Supriya and Prabin headed up the terrace and through the narrow spiral staircase into the makeshift crow's nest—a semiconstructed room with French windows, a yet-unpaved floor, and two bamboo chairs—to savor half an hour's view of Gangtok before darkness shrouded it.

"Look at the priest's paunch," Prabin said, pointing to a slouched figure slinking through the crowds. "It's getting bigger and bigger."

The priest returned everyone's greeting and paused to make small talk.

"Yes, he's a fatty," Supriya said with a giggle. "He must eat a lot of *laddoos.*"

"That he does. Who can resist *laddoos*? Even I eat five of them in one sitting."

"You should become a priest, then," Supriya said, and then serious, she asked, "Why doesn't that beggar we see on our way to school become a priest? Then he wouldn't have to beg for food."

"Well, to be a priest, one needs to be a Brahmin, like us. Not everyone can become a priest. The old man there is a Brahmin— look at him; he has been scratching his butt for three minutes."

"Does that mean he's stingy?" Supriya asked, acknowledging her father's observation with a smile but straying away from it.

"What do you mean?" Prabin questioned.

"Aren't all Brahmins stingy?"

"Do you think we are stingy?"

"No, I don't think we are, but we have another Brahmin in class, and my friends say she's a stingy Brahmin. '*Lobhi* Baahun,' they call her."

"Your classmates are six years old. They shouldn't be talking about all that."

"But Pooja is stingy. Last week, even Ms. Lhamu scolded her for not lending her eraser to Denka."

"All girls are stupid, Supriya," Prabin said with a deliberate edge in his voice.

"I am not stupid," Supriya retorted. "Ms. Lhamu is not. Mua might be, but my friends are not, and we are all girls."

"See, not all girls are stupid. Not all boys are strong. Not all Brahmins are stingy."

"I am stronger than Ramesh although he's seven."

"Not all old people are slow. Not all Bengalis are intelligent. Not all Brahmins are stingy."

Supriya didn't seem entirely convinced. "Who among my friends are Brahmins, Bua?"

"What is Avasti's last name?"

"Pradhan. Avasti Pradhan."

"No, she's not a Brahmin. Raghav Neupaney's daughter— what's her name—is a Brahmin."

"Richa. But Richa is a Christian. She goes to church. Can Christians be Brahmins?"

"She was born Brahmin. Her family converted midway."

"Oh, so even I can be a Christian if I want to?"

"Yes, you can. You can choose to be a Christian or even a Muslim, but why would you? No one can become a Brahmin unless they are born a Brahmin."

"Are we better than everyone?"

"Yes, we are the best, the very best. You should be proud you were born a Brahmin."

"How is one born Brahmin?"

"Your parents have to be Brahmins, their parents have to be Brahmins, and their parents have to be Brahmins. And their parents and their grandparents and their great-grandparents."

Supriya pulled her sweater tighter around her. This had been the coldest October in years.

"So if Avasti and I get married, will our baby be a Brahmin?"

Before Prabin could figure out a suitable answer, his wife, Khusboo, called from downstairs. It was time for Supriya to go to bed.

Early the next morning, right after she woke up, Supriya headed to Prabin's room and snuggled up to him for a few minutes. She did this every school day. Khusboo left for her morning lectures before anyone rose.

"So what did you dream of?" Prabin asked her.

"I don't know," Supriya said groggily, the edges of her lips trying hard not to betray a smile. "Ghosts."

"The scary ones or the sari ones?"

"This one was different. She wore a sari, but her face was scary."

"That means she was a clown, not a ghost. Or it was a two-in-one ghost."

"Except this one said she would eat you."

"What did you ask her to do?"

"I told her you were old and unhealthy. Mua was juicier. She could eat her."

"You naughty girl. Wait until I tell Mua. Now get up. It's time to brush your teeth."

"Why don't I get my bed tea like you do?"

"Because only grown-ups drink tea."

"But at Dolma's place, when she said she wanted to drink wine, her father said she wasn't old enough to drink wine, so she should stick to tea."

"Dolma will probably get a mustache soon, like your friend . . ." He searched for the name.

"Resha. Your memory is worse than Mua's. I am the smartest in the family."

"Yes, that's her name. Will we brush now?"

"I think Resha is a boy. Her parents must have wanted a girl, so they dress her up as a girl."

"And what makes you think a six-year-old boy would have a mustache?" Prabin asked, getting up, and tugging at the edge of his daughter's blanket.

"Yes, how would I know?" Supriya said, following Prabin to the bathroom, where he had already squeezed out the tooth-paste on her brush. "I don't play with any boys but Ramesh. And Ramesh is like a girl. I beat him at rubber band twice."

They walked to Tashi Namgyal Academy, about a kilometer uphill, hand in hand, immersed in deep conversation, oblivious to the world around them, forcing onlookers to smile and acknowledge the inadequacies of their own relationships. Prabin returned someone's greeting with barely disguised irritation. It was obvious to the greeter he was disrupting something serious. The daughter smiled and looked up to the father when she talked. She listened with rapt attention when he talked. She laughed when he said something. He laughed louder at her jokes. The townspeople would have paid money for a snippet of this conversation. It was a beautiful picture: Prabin, tall, fair, aquiline-nosed, and Supriya, fairer, smiling, always happy, her cherubic face straight from a children's catalog.

"But the kurta Ms. Lhamu wore yesterday was pink," Supriya said through a gap where most of her teeth were until recently. "I told you she always wears pink on Thursdays."

"Yes, but wasn't it her birthday yesterday?" Prabin said, shifting the weight of Supriya's backpack from his left shoulder to right. "I thought she'd wear her birthday kurta."

"Yes, because adults buy new clothes on their birthdays like you and Mua always do." Supriya laughed. "You always buy new clothes."

"Maybe we should start buying clothes. Look at my track pants. Do you see a hole?"

"Are we becoming poor, Bua?" She was serious. "Is that why you don't buy new clothes?"

"No, no, remember how I've told you about the various properties we have? And the bookstore? And Mua's job? And the rent from the *Kaiyas* downstairs. We are not poor."

"You called them *Kaiyas*." She laughed. "Bad word, bad word. Uneducated word."

"Oh, sorry, I shouldn't have."

"So are we *arabpatis* then?"

"No, we aren't billionaires."

"*Crorepatis*?"

"Not really."

"*Lakhapatis*? Millionaires?"

"Maybe."

By now she was in stitches. "*Hajarpatis*?"

"Perhaps."

"Ha, ha. Even I am a *hajarpati*. I have 8,900 rupees in the bank. That's almost 10,000. I wouldn't be a *lakhapati* if I had 10,000, right?"

"No, you would need ten more 10,000s for a lakh."

"Ten? Okay. The math they teach at school is so easy. My friends don't even know of five-, six- and seven-digit numerals."

"And you know everything, don't you?"

"Well, I am smarter than everyone. I think I am smarter than Mua, too."

"I wonder how hurt she'd feel if she found out we talk about her," Prabin said in all seriousness.

"But she won't. Unless I tell her about it the day I get mad at you."

"Why would you get mad at me? What do I have to do for you to get mad at me?"

"Oh, you never know," Supriya said with feigned exasperation.

When they reached the gate of Tashi Namgyal Academy, where two of her friends waited for her, Supriya took the backpack from her father and clung to his leg in a gesture of mock emotion they both loved. She then asked him if he would pick her up. He'd always say he wouldn't but Mua would, and she'd contort her face in hurt before heading to her waiting friends. It was a recurring routine.

His bookstore on MG Marg, a rented space a stone's throw away from where they lived, made a huge profit and, although he had two efficient and honest helpers there, he liked being at work early in the morning. During lunch, one of his servants arrived with his lunch box and daughter. Khusboo picked his daughter up from school, fed her at home, got her changed into something frilly and sent her to the store with the servant. Father and daughter then spent time reading books, looking at pictures, and talking. Supriya sat on a stack of hardcover encyclopedias holding court with the two helpers and anyone who was in the store. When the math involved wasn't too taxing, Prabin asked her to handle change as the customers smiled indulgently and said a word of praise or two. He was too busy to read a Hans Christian Andersen story to her today, so she took over and read the book out loud, occasionally stumbling and pausing, again ingratiating herself with the customers with a showmanship that improved with each passing day.

"How is she?" he asked his wife when she finally came to the living room after what seemed like hours.

"Asleep." Khusboo looked exhausted.

"I had no idea she'd grow this fast." He had difficulty holding himself back.

"She's a girl. It happens to all of them."

"But only yesterday she was cuddling with me. She was a little girl."

"She's a woman now. We both need to get used to it."

"Did you think it would happen this early?" He was tearing up.

"Yes, she's twelve. I was a bit worried she hadn't had it until now. Wasn't your mother married at fourteen?"

"You could've warned me." A pause followed every word.

"I thought you already knew. You told me she had stopped coming to your bed in the mornings, and you also sat as far from her as you could when watching TV. I thought you knew."

But Prabin hadn't. Had he known, the knowledge would have helped him prepare for this in some way. He hadn't given his daughter's coming of age much thought, and he hadn't expected it would affect him the way it did. He was angry with himself for letting a perfectly normal biological process bother him.

The snuggle routine, which started with Supriya's heading from her bed and jumping into his early in the morning, had stopped a year ago, heralding a new phase in their relationship. The hugs, kisses, and easy physical comfort graduated to high-fives, thumbs-ups, and a spatial awareness Prabin hadn't quite noticed evolve.

Wanting to clear his head, Prabin went to the top of the building and tended to flowers in earthen pots. The orchids and azaleas were in full April bloom, and the crow's nest, with its recently added marble floor and rug, was more of an oasis to him than ever before. Looking down four stories—the remaining three floors were below road level—he was filled with a sense of accomplishment. A momentary happiness enveloped him when a picture of Supriya taken during her naming ceremony brought him to reality. He realized he had barely exchanged a word with his daughter the past few weeks.

Several days later, Supriya asked her mother if she could spend a night at Avasti's place. Prabin didn't know about it until Khusboo brought it up late at night. When he expressed confusion and hurt at not having been the one his daughter sought permission from, Khusboo explained that Supriya probably asked her because mother and daughter had been home at the same time while Prabin was at the store. The reasoning did little to reassure Prabin.

The next morning, he found Supriya at the dining table, her head buried in a *Femina*. He seldom saw her in the mornings these days. She woke up late, really late, bathed no matter how cold the day, and often rushed out without eating breakfast. They had stopped walking together to school, and as much as Prabin missed it, he attributed it to her growing up. That, though, was just the beginning of a series of changes. A lot had gone on after.

"Sleepover?" he asked.

"Um." Supriya didn't bother looking up.

"Why didn't you ask me?"

"I am going to be late." Supriya clutched her backpack and didn't look at him.

"We need to talk."

"I am late." She headed for the door.

"We don't talk at all these days. I persuaded your mother to allow you to continue swimming. I didn't even receive a thanks for that."

"Maybe I will make you a card. And bake you a cake. And let the neighbors know you're the best father in the world."

"You're raising your voice. It's loud enough for the tenants downstairs to hear you."

"I can't whisper to you," Supriya hissed. "Not when you're causing me to be late for school."

"We'll talk about it later," said Prabin, his voice suddenly soft. "I will be waiting for you. I'll be back from the store before you're back from school."

Supriya betrayed no emotion. Within a second, she was gone.

Prabin didn't go to the bookstore that day. He wanted to be home when Supriya arrived. Khusboo returned from college and, sensing he wasn't in the best mood, asked him if he might want to join her for shopping. Prabin replied that he wanted to be left alone.

The wait for Supriya turned out to be longer than anticipated. She finally walked in at about four, her shirt untucked and her stockings rolled down.

"You're late," Prabin said the moment she walked in.

A smirk greeted him.

"I told you I'd be waiting."

"Wow! What an honor. The man of the house waits for my arrival."

"When did you learn to speak that way, my dear?" Prabin was aware of his raised voice and tried compensating by being extra-polite.

"When you were away at the store," said Supriya. And with a catch in the voice, she added, "You know, when you weren't there for me, you hypocrite."

Prabin was silent. He wanted to know what the issue was.

"What have I done, Supriya?" he asked—sadly, softly—looking her in the eye. "We've become strangers here. I haven't spoken to you in days. Whatever happened to all the talks about school, the secrets, and your life? You tell me nothing these days."

"And what do you tell me, Bua? You don't even sit on the same sofa as me."

Prabin didn't know how to deflect the accusation. He thought of something to say, but his daughter didn't allow him.

"Ever since I had my period, you've become an entirely different person. You locked me in the room for seven days after. Mua told me I couldn't see the sun, that I couldn't see a man's face. All those days there, I cried. I cried because I felt guilty, because I thought I had committed a sin. I'd look at myself in the mirror and hate myself. I honestly thought I was an evil person, or that I had done something bad. My body hurt, and so did my thoughts. When I confided in a teacher at school, she said I might have been depressed. Seven days in a room, Bua."

This wasn't his twelve-year-old girl speaking. The voice wasn't hers. His little girl was talking like a woman who had matured, gained perspective, and had realized her sex held a secondary place in her community. He had never brought her up that way. Man or woman, girl or boy—they were all equal, and that's what he had taught her. He was about to gently tell her that she did have Mua for company, but bawls now replaced Supriya's sobs, and she gave him no opportunity.

"Mua told me all about it—all about periods." The sputters were back. "I knew about them. I've always known. I am smarter than anyone my age. Pooja kept it hidden from her parents for six months. I should have kept mine a secret from you people, too. Had I known I'd be imprisoned in my own room, I'd have never told her. I thought you'd understand at least. I thought you'd help me out. But you didn't. You are no different from others. What an idiot I was to hope you'd one day show up and tell me I'd always be your little one."

"There's nothing wrong with periods, Supriya. Everyone—every female—has them."

"I know, you fool," Supriya screamed, quiet sniffles punctuating her speech. "I know everyone has them. But you could have at least come into my room to talk. You could have said what you just said. You could have laughed about it. You could have made it normal. There I was, thinking it was the end of the world, and you . . . you didn't care at all. You didn't even pop your head into my room to say hello. And all along I thought you'd tell me Mua is a fool, and we'd go up to the terrace and laugh about it all. When even you treated me like I was an animal—no, worse than that—I really thought I had done something wrong. I hated myself. I hated you. I hated life. I'd get these pains in my stomach, not knowing where they came from. I'd feel woozy one minute and get cramps the next. I hate you."

Supriya cried for a long time. She'd stop for a while, awaken some memory from her week-long lockdown and start to sob. Prabin wanted to go to her, hold her in his arms and run his hands down her hair, but he couldn't. He also wanted to cry but knew, for his daughter's sake, he shouldn't.

"I am sorry, Supriya. I wish I had known what you went through. See, I am a man, after all. I don't know so much. But that's no excuse. I was a fool to think you'd be all right in that room for seven days. I think it's a stupid tradition, I do, but Mua thinks it's important. Had I known it would be this difficult on you, I'd never have allowed her to go through with it. I am sorry, Supriya, please understand how sorry I am."

"Bua." She was walking toward her room, her voice breaking into sobs again.

"Yes?" he asked hopefully. He walked toward her. He was going to hug her no matter what. It had been too long.

"I'll never forgive you for this," she said, her voice a tremor, as she closed the door.

Khusboo didn't like the decision, and she made no effort to hide it.

"A beauty pageant?" she said. "What will people say? I've tried my best to talk to her, but why would she listen to me? There might even be a swimsuit round. And this is just a regional competition. Regional competitions are cheap; they hardly have the same prestige as Ms. India."

"She's a beauty, our daughter," Prabin said without looking away from the game of solitaire on the screen.

The crow's nest had been hooked up with a computer and the Internet just a few months ago despite Khusboo's repeated insistence that the study was a better choice. Prabin had argued that working on the computer while watching the town from high up was more inspiring, and when she saw he wouldn't have had it any other way, she relented. Supriya didn't have an opinion because she was already away in college in Kolkata and only used her laptop.

"Doesn't mean she has to prove it to the world by participating in a beauty contest," Khusboo retorted. "My parents are illiterate, and so is your mother. Think of what they will say when they find out our Supriya is parading around half naked in a swimsuit."

"We aren't even sure if there will be a swimsuit competition, Khusboo, and even if there is, you need to grow with the times. Let her do what she wants. It might be good for her—think of the exposure she will receive."

"Of course, she convinced you. You think everything she does is okay. One of these days, she'll elope, and you'll think that's okay, too."

"Why not? She can tell us if she wants to get married to someone. Why would she elope? We aren't Rais, you know."

"And if she marries a Rai?"

"Let her. Times have changed, Khusboo. Let her marry whom she chooses."

"No one from my side of the family has married a non-Brahmin—just one *Jaisi*. That's it. And we can't allow our daughter to marry anyone but a Brahmin. All your grandiose plans of caste equality do not apply to your daughter. And this isn't an illiterate woman speaking. I teach about problems inter-caste marriages cause. I have seen them in front of my eyes. The *Matwalis*, they dip their thumb in alcohol and have their newborn babies suck on it. Imagine that being done to your grandson."

"Horrifying," Prabin said. Solitaire required too little concentration to blank his wife out completely.

"Not serious at all, as always. She's eighteen. Most girls in our family get married around twenty-three. We want to make sure she's not serious with anyone."

"So she cannot be serious with boys and just date, then? Is that what you're trying to say?"

"Shut up. You have stopped respecting the *janaai*. You make fun of it like it isn't a sacred thread anymore. Didn't you also tell the driver you've stopped wearing it? At least don't advertise it to anyone. It's insulting. If a Brahmin stops wearing it, the Chettris will, too."

"All right, I'll wear the *janaai* tomorrow. And I don't mind if my daughter gets married to a non-Brahmin. Rai, Tamang, Limbu, Tibetan—I am okay with them all."

"Ah, you must be looking forward to having grandchildren with pig-like noses."

"At least they won't have hawk-like noses that start from the top of their heads." He added: "Like you do."

It was true, Prabin admitted to himself, when Khusboo finally left him alone, that he didn't care so much about what caste his future son-in-law belonged to. He wasn't aware of how

his friends' and brothers' marriages worked, but he knew his
marriage wasn't a resounding success. He didn't hate his wife
or love her. He belonged to a generation that didn't talk about
issues like love and romance openly, although he was sure
everyone thought about them. He and his wife were used to
each other. Like the bamboo chair in the crow's nest he was sitting on, his wife was a part of the house, and in that extension,
a part of him. He felt for her when her back problems bothered
her, but he felt for the servant, too, when the old man coughed
all night long.

Khusboo and he didn't sleep together—she slept on a mat-
tress on the floor to help reduce her backache—and intimacy
now was an awkward topic. Sometimes Prabin wondered how
he would be affected if his wife died or, worse, if she left him,
and concluded his life wouldn't change so much after all. With
Khusboo's going to college before he woke up and his leaving
for the store for ten-hour shifts before she returned, they didn't
even spend much time together. And he liked it that way; he
suspected she felt the same way. On the rare occasions they
were home at the same time, like Sundays and holidays,
they kept conversation to a minimum, their common platform
being their daughter.

If this is what an arranged marriage felt like—dull, constrict-
ing, suffocating—he didn't wish it on his daughter. He wanted
his daughter to live, something he felt he hadn't done fully, to
experience life with a partner as hungry for life as she was,
to travel, to see the world, to be deeply in love . . .

His thoughts were interrupted by the phone ringing. It was
Supriya.

"What did she say?" she asked.

"Not very happy," he sing-sang. "Not very happy."

"I knew it. What exactly did she say?"

"Family. Swimsuit. People."

"There may not even be a swimwear round. Trust her to make it dramatic. Where's she now?"

"Don't know. I am upstairs."

"Think you can persuade her to come around?"

"She'll be fine. Don't worry about it."

"And you, are you all right with it?" Her voice changed.

He detected the apprehension. "Totally."

"Okay, your answer came too fast. Are you absolutely okay with it?"

"I am. Believe me, I am."

"Even the swimwear?"

"I'd much rather there not be a swimwear round, but I don't think it's an issue."

"Will you come see me compete?"

"I wouldn't miss it for the world."

"Even if Mua doesn't come?"

"Don't worry, she will come."

"To be honest, I'll be happy if one of you is here. It'd be an added bonus if both of you came."

"We'll both be there."

"All right, then, see you soon. Text me if she says anything too funny or nasty."

"She said you'd elope if I continued allowing you to do what you want."

"Why would I elope? I'll proudly march the man I will marry to the house in full view of the entire Gangtok bazaar."

"Just what I told her. Even the Laal Bazaar?"

"As well as Battis Mile. Okay, no minutes, got to go. Bye. Don't tell her I asked you anything."

"Goodnight."

He was beaming when he hung up.

Supriya called him two days later to declare she was not going to compete after all. She said she had to choose between

rehearsing for the competition or going to Europe on an edu-
cational tour, and because Europe was a childhood dream, she
chose the latter. Prabin asked his daughter, paying little heed
to the glare coming from his wife's direction, if she could do
Europe some other time, but Supriya said she couldn't wait.
And, besides, she could always participate in the pageant
next year.

"Tell Mua I didn't do it because of the mandatory swimsuit
round," she said. "How could I do that to my family? Dissolve its
respect in mud, you know."

"I will. She's here actually. Speak to her."

He handed the phone to Khusboo.

"Okay, okay, okay," Khusboo said, victoriously taking it all
in. "Well, thank you. Thanks. Good. Yes, I know. No one can
talk now. And you can begin eating, too. Europe? Will that be
expensive? Okay, okay, okay, oh, your savings? No, no, I will ask
Bua if we can finance you. You don't need to touch the money
you've been saving since four. All right, bye."

Khusboo placed the receiver back on the cradle.

"She probably didn't get selected." She maliciously smiled.
"She thinks I am a fool—like I'll believe she didn't take part for
me. And what a nice gateway for the Europe trip—no one asks
her a thing about it."

"But she said she'd pay for it with her own money," Prabin
said in his daughter's defense.

"Will you allow her to?" his wife asked, trying her best to
catch the fly nervously fluttering around the screens that went
with their windows.

"No, of course, not," Prabin said, mildly piqued. "As you said,
she's been saving since she was four."

"She knew that's what we would say." She looked at him conspiratorially as she caught the fly, took it out to the balcony and
let it free.

Prabin couldn't help noticing how similar his wife was to the insect in the window. The fly darted in and out, just like she did, and he paid both no mind. Every so often, though, it irritated him so much that he was tempted to squish it, just like he wanted to throttle his wife right now. She didn't hurt the fly; hurting his wife right now would not be in keeping with the warped metaphor he had just concocted. She'd always think their daughter was up to no good. If that's what gives her life a purpose, let her be, Prabin thought as he headed to the store.

At twenty-four, Supriya brought her boyfriend home for the first time. They had been together for three years, but Supriya had made it clear to Prabin that it was a relationship going nowhere, a fact that simultaneously disconcerted and relieved her mother.

"*Abbui*, a Pradhan," she had remarked to Prabin after Supriya's call. "Thank God there's no intention of marriage. But why does she need to bring him home? We'll tell anyone who asks he's her *Rakhi* brother."

Anwesh Pradhan, Prabin reasoned, wasn't such a bad boy. He spoke well, was respectable, seemed like he was from an excellent family, had received a better education than his daughter had (St. Paul's, Darjeeling; Bishop Cotton, Bangalore; St. Stephen's, Delhi; JNU, Delhi) and was an overall likable man. For a little while he was baffled why his daughter did not think of him as the marrying kind. He had only to ask the next question.

"What do you intend to do with a degree in political science, Ashish?" he asked. Khusboo did very little talking. She hadn't even cooked anything special.

"The name is Anwesh, Bua," Supriya corrected him with a pat on his head and went on a verbal trip down memory lane, rife with anecdotes that sprang from his name-forgetting ways.

"Politics, Uncle," Anwesh said, unflustered. "I am already in the GJM. I like Bimal Gurung's leadership, but some day, I hope to be the next Bimal Gurung. Subash Ghisingh did nothing for the Darjeeling district. So many years later, we're still not a state. I worked very closely with Jaswant Singh's campaign and now understand how the grassroots level works. I think he's the one who'll get us out of this quandary."

"But Jaswant Singh was expelled from his own party," Prabin interrupted. "He doesn't even know what's going to happen tomorrow."

"He'll join Congress, Uncle, and Congress will easily free Gorkhaland. We'll no longer be under the oppressive regime of Kolkata. Just you see."

They finished dinner and went to the crow's nest without Khusboo. Just a week ago, Prabin had installed a minibar in one corner. He poured himself a whiskey, the local brand, and asked Anwesh and Supriya to help themselves. Anwesh made himself a drink by adding a little whiskey to his glass and brimming it with water. Supriya declined.

"So what do you want to do for a career, Anwesh?" He got the name right.

"Politics, Uncle, will be my career. I will see to it that the Darjeeling Gorkha Hill Council will be free and continue serving in some political capacity."

"Do you see yourself as a DGHC minister if it becomes a state one day, Anwesh?" He purposefully avoided calling him "son."

"Yes, Uncle, I do. I will become the chief minister one day. Your daughter thinks it's impossible, though. She thinks I am wasting my time."

"Did you say that, Supriya?" Prabin asked, not looking at anyone, or anything, in particular.

"Yes, I did," Supriya said. "And that's the reason I won't marry you, Anwesh."

"Just give me five years, Supriya. Five years is all I need."

"No, Anwesh, I gave you two, and you still don't have a job or money of your own. You're still dependent on your parents for money. We've talked about this before."

Prabin fidgeted uncomfortably in his seat, shuffling his liquor from one hand to another. He asked if he should leave.

"No, that's fine, Bua, we're having a casual discussion," Supriya said. "Look at us—still smiling."

She was smiling; Anwesh wasn't.

"I will not get married to someone who makes less money than I do," Supriya said.

"You're insulting me, Supriya." The howling of a pack of stray dogs drowned Anwesh's voice. "I keep telling you to give me five years to prove myself."

"You don't need five years to prove yourself. I wouldn't mind your political *gundagiri* at all if only you had a job. You could teach in a college somewhere and continue to mobilize the youth. You could work someplace—that would put your education to good use."

Her father stood up to leave, but so did Anwesh.

"I guess this means I should leave?" Anwesh asked.

"Probably," Supriya said. "Good luck."

"All right, Uncle, thank you so much for dinner," Anwesh said. "Namaste."

"Goodnight, Anwesh," Prabin said.

"I'll see you to the door." Supriya led the way.

Prabin had expected some talk to take place downstairs and was surprised when Supriya returned immediately.

"Wow," he remarked.

"I know," she said. "He wouldn't have left me alone had I not insulted him here."

Prabin smiled. "So that's why you brought him here?"

"Well, yes, he knows how much you mean to me, and to impress you was his biggest goal. After the DGHC nonsense, of course. It all went downhill when I brought up finance and independence issues."

"Wow," Prabin remarked. "I don't know what to say."

"I know. There's not a lot for you to say."

"Do you think you'll ever see him again?"

"I don't know."

"He seemed pretty shaken."

"Must have been the drink—you know, with four-fifths water."

He figured she was trying to make light of the situation. "These Darjeeling people—I love the way they speak."

"I know. And what they say about St. Paul's products not being able to mingle is certainly true."

"He seemed social enough."

"He rehearsed for this meeting a million times. Where do you think the book on how to run a successful business and the bouquet for Mua came from?"

"Did you see her face when he handed her the flowers?" They were back to their chitchat. "I had difficulty controlling my laughter. To be honest, I was a little insulted he brought me a book on how to manage my business. You probably told him I don't manage the bookstore well enough."

"Yes, he tried. But giving a book like that to the most successful bookstore owner in town is a little silly, I agree."

"You know everyone says we are more successful than Good Books," Prabin boasted. "Now we just have to beat Rachna Books."

"Weren't you always?" Supriya teased. "Or were those lies to appease my childish questions about who had more money, who was bigger, and who was more powerful?"

"Be absolutely honest with me, Supriya. You couldn't have turned down the man simply because you didn't like the idea of his being in politics. There's something about Anwesh that convinces anyone he meets he's going to do great things. I'll give it in writing that he will be a great man. There's more to it than his involvement in politics."

"Yes, there is," she replied, looking straight ahead.

"Is there someone else?"

"No, not at all."

"Then why?"

"He's not a Brahmin, Bua. Remember to be a Brahmin, both your parents need to be Brahmins? I want my children to be Brahmin."

"Yes, *chulhai nimto*—of course, everyone's invited," Khusboo said on the phone. "Yes, bring the children, too. How often do they get to feast on arranged marriages these days? They need to know that they should get married to someone of their own caste. This will be an example. What? *Aye*, no, no, it's not entirely arranged. Who goes for totally arranged marriages these days? But he's a Brahmin, the upper berth, and yes, the *kundalis* match perfectly. Ten out of ten, the pundit says. She's thirty, and he's thirty-one. Perfect. Thank you, thank you. All right, we'll see you at the wedding then. Let's wear something understated and elegant. We need to show them the girl's side is educated and classy, you know. Bye."

Supriya and Prabin were addressing invitations—he in Nepali, and she in English—and rolled their eyes while nodding their heads in disbelief when Khusboo brought up the issue of the groom's being a Brahmin and the perfectly harmonious birth charts. Supriya wouldn't allow her birth chart to be read, and Khusboo had to acquiesce because Supriya had done her the biggest favor of all by getting married to a Brahmin. All these years, Prabin hadn't disclosed to his wife their daughter's desire to get married to a man from her caste. He often considered telling her about what transpired in the crow's nest after

Anwesh's dismissal six years ago. Something stopped him. He felt petty hiding a matter that would have possibly saved his wife six years of fitful sleep, but he didn't mention a thing. It was his little secret, and he knew why.

He didn't want his wife to relax while he still tossed and turned. Letting her know that Supriya was not getting married to anyone but a Brahmin would be the end of her worries. It, however, wouldn't be the end of his. What if her husband, a righteous Brahmin in every way, ended up treating his daughter the way he, Prabin, treated his wife? What if Supriya's evolved into a marriage deprived of love like his was? Yes, he didn't cheat on his wife, and he knew she didn't cheat on him, but neither gave the other the happiness one expects from a spouse. Days went by without their having exchanged a word with each other. All the joy that came from their marriage resided in their daughter. And he didn't wish that life for his daughter. God knows he had failed as a husband; he didn't want another man like him, the picture-perfect Brahmin, to fail Supriya. He knew his reasons for keeping Supriya's desire a secret were selfish, inhumane even, but he couldn't imagine being the lone suffering person.

"All Nepali cards are ready, right?" Khusboo asked.

"Yes, they are," Prabin said. "Finally. I still don't understand why we are inviting this many people."

"I told you I wanted a court wedding," Supriya said. "You could have given the money to me to buy a house."

"What an inappropriate thing to say," Khusboo shouted. "Everything we have is yours. Will we take all our money with us when we die or what? Your husband isn't exactly a poor man. And he's already a deputy secretary in the government now. You're bound to get a government job in no time. What a lucky girl."

"She doesn't want a government job, Khusboo," Prabin said, inviting a pinch from Supriya. He looked forward to the battle that would ensue.

"Ah! The Acharyas," Khusboo said. "Supriya Acharya."

"She doesn't want to change her last name," Prabin quipped, once again hoping he had instigated a quarrel.

Supriya's phone rang. It was Sahil, her fiancé, and she went to her room.

Supriya had made Prabin aware of Sahil some time ago.

She called him one day, asked him if he was alone, and said she had something to share.

"His name is Sahil, and he's a Baahun."

"Oh, good, I don't need to know more, of course," Prabin joked.

"Good family. A good job. A great personality. Good character."

"All right." He gave her the signal to continue.

"Only son." She laughed. "Sister is in the US. No flirtatious brothers-in-law to worry about."

"He seems perfect in every way. There must be something negative about him."

"Um, not that I can think of."

"C'mon, something."

"No, none whatsoever."

"Okay, if not negative, something you don't like."

"He wears contacts and keeps losing them."

"Is that it?"

"Hold on."

"Sure."

"Let me think." She repeated herself.

"Well, if we are nitpicking, he drinks moderately. And he tends to get drunk rather fast."

"Do you think that's serious?"

"Well, I tell him that I love him all the time except when he drinks."

"What do you want to do when he drinks?"

"Kill him," she said. "But it doesn't worry me so much. He doesn't go out drinking every night."

"Not a wife beater in the making?"

"No, about that I am sure."

"Alcoholic?"

"The reality of alcoholism is different for us than it's for you, Bua. All young people drink."

"So do I."

"Yes, and Mua thinks you're an alcoholic. See my point?"

"I do."

The first time they met him, both husband and wife fell for Sahil. He was suave, tall, very good looking, had impeccable manners, and made excellent conversation. For the first time in years, Prabin and Khusboo talked for some time before they went to bed. Sahil was a charmer. A sincere charmer, they both agreed. And he seemed very into their daughter, who was now back in the room, laughing on the phone at something he had just said.

"He's coming for your birthday," Supriya yelled. "It was supposed to be a surprise, but you know surprises are never surprising, so I am letting you know. Pretend to be surprised."

"Oh, all right, so there'll be cake cutting then?" Prabin asked.

"And new clothes. Those track pants have holes in them."

"Maybe we are getting richer, Supriya."

"I know. Richer than the *Kaiyas* downstairs at least."

Sahil arrived the next day with bottles of champagne, a cake, and a present for Prabin. The wedding was three weeks later, so the trip wasn't necessary, which touched Prabin. Up in the crow's nest, his favorite place in the world, they, along with a group of a dozen close friends and relatives, toasted his sixty years, his longevity, the wedding, Khusboo's cooking skills—the vegetable pakoras and koftas she was passing around as appetizers were delicious—and a happy life. Soon, everyone downed flutes of champagne while Khusboo watched indulgently and saw to it all the plates were replenished. She was a happy woman these days.

People filled out into the terrace. Trays of lit coal dangling in the four corners of the rooftop kept them warm in the December cold. Khusboo's sister wanted to dance, and the Bollywood music blaring from the stereo persuaded all to their feet. Prabin looked around himself in satisfaction. It had been a good sixty years.

As though reading his thoughts, his daughter stopped dancing and walked up to him.

"Not a bad innings, huh?" She used a cricket term.

"Not at all." The music blared, a 2009 Bollywood hit.

"Not dancing?"

"You know how I feel about it." The music carried on as cheers from the revelers doubled.

"What about at least standing around and clapping?"

"I don't know. I'll look like an idiot."

"It's your birthday. No one cares."

"How're you feeling?" Prabin asked.

"I hate it when he drinks. Look at him making a fool of himself."

"But you always knew that, didn't you?"

"Yes, but he's these people's future son-in-law. Look at them laughing at him."

"Ah, c'mon, they're laughing with him."

"No, Bua, they are pretending. They'll probably go home and complain about your alcoholic son-in-law."

"Is he?"

"What?"

"An alcoholic. Is he an alcoholic?"

"He drinks, Bua. Every so often."

"Then why are you afraid of what people perceive of him? When did you ever care about what people think?"

"This is different, Bua."

Prabin saw Sahil tinker with the stereo. Women's laughter peppered the silence. Shakira filled the air.

"*Chyaa*, English," someone screamed.

"Yes, English—that too a vulgar one," another chimed. Laughter followed.

"Our son-in-law is making us women with no character," Khusboo's sister said.

"Why is it different now, Supriya?"

Sahil kept moving from woman to woman. Those who weren't dancing, like Khusboo, he tried carrying to the dance area. People around him shouted and clapped in encouragement while he lost his balance and came down, legs and arms entwined, with his future mother-in-law. Half the onlookers were amused, and half were scandalized. Khusboo hurriedly gathered herself while an inebriated Sahil lay on the ground laughing. He was having a good time.

"I don't know, Bua, but look at that." Supriya didn't look at Sahil. She pointed at the computer. Prabin had taught her this time-tested method of talking about people without making it too obvious who was being spoken about.

"You're getting married in weeks. You don't seem very happy, Supriya."

"I am, Bua, I swear to God, I am. It's just that when this happens, I hate him."

Sahil was up by now, and he was running around the terrace in circles with Supriya's mysteriously procured twenty-five-year-old water bottle around his neck. His speed increased with every round. The few guests who were amused earlier were now quiet. Prabin saw eyes talking and heard hushed whispers.

"Do you ever miss Anwesh?"

"Don't do this to me, Bua."

"I am just curious. You don't have to answer the question if you don't want to."

"He wasn't much of a drinker."

People began clustering around the buffet on the terrace.

"Where's the birthday boy?" someone asked. "Shouldn't he be eating?"

Prabin paid the man no attention.

"Do you think you should have a talk with him, Supriya?"

"You've no idea how many talks there have been."

A plate came crashing down. It was Sahil.

"*Mazel Tov*," he screamed.

No one knew what to do with that.

"There should probably be one more," Prabin said.

"You don't like him, do you, Bua?"

"I didn't say that, Supriya."

"You don't need to." She was crying now. "Your voice says it. Your body language says it."

"He's a good boy."

"You could have told me sooner that you didn't think we were a good match." The tears were back.

"Supriya, I never said he wasn't a good match," said Prabin. "I think you're capable of choosing someone good enough for you."

Prabin turned his attention to Sahil picking up chicken drumsticks from different plates. After having collected six pieces, he mumbled something about a game, threw the drumsticks up in the air and yelled at people for not catching them. Khusboo looked like she was about to faint.

"Anwesh would never have done this," Supriya said, wiping her tears. She forced a smile at someone and headed for the buffet.

Prabin knew he should resist saying it, but he couldn't help himself. "It's still your choice."

Supriya didn't look back at him.

The clock chimed midnight soon after their dinner. The drinking had stopped for everyone but Sahil. Prabin had carefully hidden his strong brandy under the computer desk but discovered that Sahil had excavated it. An exhausted Khusboo brought the cake with sixty candles. It took Prabin two minutes to blow them out. After he cut the cake, Sahil demanded to rub the cake on Prabin's face. This wouldn't have been a ridiculous proposition had Sahil been in a position to string his words together, but he wasn't, and Prabin quietly asked Khusboo to give him some water.

"Lie down, Sahil *jwaai saab*," Prabin said.

"Cake first, cake first," Sahil mumbled and made for the cake with his hand.

After digging out a handful, he turned to Supriya. His shirt was unbuttoned to his navel, and he rubbed cake all over Supriya's chest, who murmured something into his ears. It wasn't the stern voice she had used with Anwesh. This voice was calm and soothing, as if Sahil were a baby. In fact, it looked like she was putting a big baby to sleep.

"Enough," Prabin said. "Enough, *jwaai saab*."

Sahil was laughing, having an excellent time.

"Enough," Prabin shouted. "I don't care about whether you're my future son-in-law—you have to leave."

Sahil's hands flailed; his eyes were bloodshot. The friends and family stood around, horrified, awkward, confused about what their roles should be.

"I don't care if a son-in-law is the next thing to God." Prabin looked around. "I'll slap his silly face if I have to."

The look on his wife's face was a mixture of disbelief and self-pity. The night had gone entirely out of control, and his future son-in-law was crazy. He went to the bathroom downstairs to get away from it all. The crow's nest was a mess of broken glasses, uneaten cake, and torn streamers.

He stayed in the bathroom for a long, long time. By the time he returned, all was quiet in the house. Everyone had either left or gone to bed. Prabin went up to the crow's nest to inspect the damage done. It would also clear his head. He didn't know what to think of the night.

The cake was everywhere: on one of the bamboo chairs—God knew where the other had gone—the computer desk, and the rug. He tiptoed to get the trash can from the terrace, careful not to step on broken glass. The terrace lights were already on. Sitting right next to the trash can, on the missing bamboo chair, was Sahil with a vapid look in his eyes, carefully licking every speck of cake from his little finger. Once finished with the little finger, he moved to the thumb. After licking his thumb clean of the cake crumbs, he moved to the middle finger. He licked it clean, sucked it, and he saw to it not a bit of cake remained. He was oblivious to the standing Prabin in the doorway. His last finger was the ring finger. When his teeth retrieved the ring, along with the cake crumbs, he sucked the engagement ring dry of the cake remains. After he had licked the last crumb of cake off his hand, he spat out the ring, looked at Prabin, mumbled "Cake, cake" and passed out there.

In the shadows lurked Supriya.

"He's a Brahmin, though, Bua, he's a Brahmin," she sputtered.

"Is he stingy?"

"Not all Brahmins are stingy. Not all women weak. Not all Bengalis are intelligent."

"Sradda is stingy, though, and she's a Brahmin."

"The name is Pooja, Bua." She smiled through her tears.

MISSED BLESSING

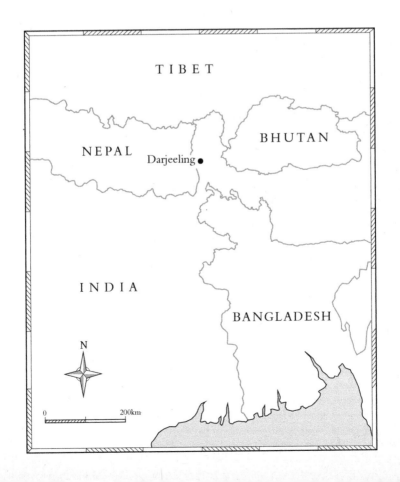

On a wall in Rajiv's four-bedded room hung pictures of all the recently deceased members of his family—his mother: blood cancer; his father: a failed liver; his father's brother and the brother's wife: a car accident; and his grandfather: old age. The *khadas*, silk scarves decking each of the frames, had turned light brown with age. The frames themselves had accumulated thick layers of dirt that the early-morning rays dancing through the windows now betrayed. Rajiv wondered aloud if his brother, who he saw was trying to go back to sleep in the bed across from him, might want to clean the frames one of these days.

"Yes, they've been neglected for too long," said his brother, Sandeep, home on his *Dashain* vacation from boarding school.

There's no way the pictures are neglected, Rajiv thought. *I begin my day looking at them and thinking about the people in them.*

He stared at his dozing brother and wished he, too, could sleep that way. His grandmother wasn't in her bed. She was probably already in the kitchen, preparing tea for him and Sandeep despite the arthritis that caused her difficulty in lifting even a small pot of water. His distant cousin, an eleven-year-old from perhaps the only family poorer than Rajiv's, wasn't in his bed either. Rajiv heard no sounds of pots clanking on the floor, so he assumed Tikam was in the kitchen doing most of the work while the old lady supervised. Tikam's bed, the smallest in the room, was already made—the quilt had been folded into a neat rectangle and set against the wall.

The missionaries would be here soon. During the past three weeks, a middle-aged couple from America had shown up at Rajiv's place at six almost every morning. They had lived in Darjeeling for a year or so, helping poor people get to know Christ. Rajiv had difficulty believing the Scotts—he called them Mr. and Ms. Scott despite their wanting to be addressed as Michael and Christa—had been around only for a year because they conversed in fluent Nepali and seemed extremely comfortable in their unfamiliar surroundings. They sat cross-legged on the floor and drank boiled water, unlike those foreign tourists who wouldn't touch any liquid that didn't come in sealed bottles. They also didn't marvel every three seconds at the beauty of Darjeeling's sunrises.

These were the first missionaries Rajiv had known intimately, and he was fond of them. He especially liked Michael, who didn't talk much, just like Rajiv's father. Christa was always in good spirits and was ready for a good, civilized debate—no voice was raised, no hot words thrown. Rajiv never found in the Scotts any of the mendacity his father was convinced characterized missionaries. The Scotts didn't sugarcoat, they didn't question his faith in Hinduism, and they seldom extolled the virtues of Jesus. It sometimes felt like they were his sounding board, a respite from the mundane cycles of his life. Their positive take on everything was inspiring, and these hourly sessions were incentive enough to get out of bed. He always found that after spending time with the couple, more so with Michael, he felt calmer, like their cheer rubbed off on him, so when Rajiv heard a knock, followed by Tikam's greeting, he sprinted to the small terrace, where he often convened with the Scotts when the weather was right.

It wasn't the Scotts. Rajiv should have known better—it was a Sunday, and they never came to his place on Sundays. Their duties at church made morning visits nearly impossible. Rajiv's *mama*, his mother's younger brother, came barging in.

"You were still sleeping," his *mama* said, lowering his glasses from the top of his bald head. "All your mother's siblings will be in Darjeeling on Friday for *Dashain*. Their families will be here, too. They will mostly be staying at my place, but you will have to make room in yours for your Manju *chema* and her daughter. Her husband is staying home so he can offer *tika* there. He's the oldest brother; it makes sense."

"How many of them will be there?"

"She and her daughter. Her husband's brother's daughter will also be there. These Shillong people love Darjeeling."

"That's three, then."

Rajiv knew who the cousin's cousin was. Her name was Niveeta, and they had met once when they were both toddlers— she had bitten him when he touched her toy rabbit, and he had had to get a tetanus shot. It was a painful childhood memory, but he found himself smiling at the absurdity of now meeting this person from his past. He wondered what she'd look like as an adult and if she remembered what she'd done to him.

"Yes, and they are leaving tomorrow. Manju *nana* has to return to Shillong because she doesn't trust her *bekaamey* husband with the house, and the girls are returning to college in Delhi. Who allows their daughters to come home during the *Dashain* vacation, I don't understand."

"You know there's no space here," Rajiv said. "All the four beds are occupied."

"Work something out. Share a bed with your brother and put some mattresses on the floor. It's festival time, and you should be open to such eventualities. If relatives don't visit one another during *Dashain,* when will they?"

"Do you know how many there will be? You know how small the room is. If they don't mind sleeping on mattresses in the kitchen, I might be able to make something happen."

"They are guests. You need to treat them well. You, your brother and the boy can sleep in the kitchen. That way, you make room for three guests in the beds and a couple more on the floor of the sitting room."

"There's no sitting room," Rajiv said.

His *mama* didn't seem to notice.

"Also, clean this place up a bit. It's always a mess."

His uncle was on his way out now. Rajiv asked him if he wanted some tea.

"That cousin of yours makes terrible tea," the older man said. "I'd be a fool to start off my day with it."

And with that, he snapped around on his heels and walked away.

Rajiv stood quiet. It was just like his *mama* to drop in unannounced this early in the morning with news like that. He wanted to tell his *mama* about his grandmother's health, about her anxiety attacks, about how he couldn't sleep well if he heard so much as a whisper. He wanted to ask his *mama* who would cook. Tikam was too young, and his grandmother was too frail to prepare a meal for her small family, let alone for guests whose numbers threatened to engender economic imbalance in the house. Rajiv was good in the kitchen, but his experience was limited to a handful of dishes. Their house probably didn't even have enough plates to feed three extra people. Rajiv dreaded the idea of asking the Scotts to lend him additional serving dishes. They would undoubtedly understand, but the humiliation of borrowing yet another thing from them was too much to bear. They had already given him an old set of chairs they said they had no use for. Asking his friends was out of question—he was too proud. He decided to share with his grandmother this bizarre development; she wouldn't have a solution, but he'd feel better if she was involved.

His grandmother was deaf in her right ear, so he had to position himself close on her left side.

"*Mama* says there might be about six of them for three days," he explained.

"And where exactly would we fit them?" the toothless lady asked. "On the terrace? Like they do in the plains?"

"This is Darjeeling, not Bagdogra. They'll freeze to death on the terrace."

"Why can't they all stay at your *mama*'s place? At least there's some space there. You know what happens when I can't sleep."

"I know, but we need to adjust. These are the same people who pooled in money so I could become an engineer."

"Yes, not that the degree has been helpful in getting you a job. You still spend all day chatting with those senseless Christians."

Years of experience had taught Rajiv not to react to any of his grandmother's prejudices. He knew she mostly meant well. It was also unwise to explain to an eighty-year-old the current job market in Darjeeling, which had a lot to do with the frequent strikes that various political parties called in an attempt to attract national attention to their demand of a separate state. The economy was crippled; opportunities were nonexistent. And he didn't want this decaying woman to know that she was the reason he hadn't left Darjeeling to go to Delhi or Bangalore for an IT job. His younger brother was in a boarding school in Mirik, and going by his dismal academic record, he would likely be there for a few more years. If Rajiv left home to pursue a career, his grandmother would be alone. The number of trips he made home from his engineering college in Majitar, in Sikkim, to take care of her had made him realize that going too far away was fatal—Bangalore wasn't a taxi ride away from Darjeeling like Majitar was. His grandmother would not be willing to move to a big city. She wanted to die in Darjeeling, in the hills, surrounded by the mountains and her people.

"I can't get a job three months after finishing college," Rajiv said. "The competition is intense."

"Weren't you the boy who always came first in his class? If they don't give you a job, who will they give it to?"

"It's *Dashain* time. All the offices are closed now, so there's no point talking about employment. We need to find a way to house all these people."

Sandeep staggered into the kitchen, combing his cowlicks.

"What people?" he said.

The grandmother filled him in.

"That's your *mama* and your mother's side of the family for you," she said. "They have no consideration for anyone."

"I could always go sleep at Sonam's place," Sandeep offered. "That's one fewer person in the house. And I could take Tikam with me."

"Tikam needs to be here to run errands," Rajiv countered. "And they will have something to say when they notice your absence. You know how they are—the house is never clean enough, the food never good enough, and we are never hospitable enough."

"Why should they stay here?" the grandmother asked. "They don't even accept *tika* from me. I am not good enough for them. A dying lady's blessings aren't important to them."

"You aren't even related to them, Boju," said Rajiv. "Why should you put *tika* on them? And they are probably uncomfortable you'll give them money with your blessings. They don't want to be a burden on you. It's no secret we don't have money."

"You're your mother's son, *naati*—you never think your family is in the wrong. If they understood our struggles, they wouldn't come to our place as guests for three whole days. No one chooses to become guests in an eighty-year-old's house if they are considerate. They know I am a sick, dying woman. They have nothing but themselves in mind."

Sandeep tapped the bottom of his glass to release the last few droplets of tea before placing it on the elevated platform in the kitchen corner that served as a sink.

"I am heading out," he said. "Does anyone need anything?"

"You never wash anything you use, just like your father," the grandmother complained. "Even those Christians who have no shame about coming here every day wash their cups."

"I'll wash the glass when I return," Sandeep said.

"That's what your father used to say, too," the grandmother said, and somewhat fondly added, "He's his father's son, a true Rai from Pankhabari—unlike his older brother."

The last time relatives from his mother's side visited, Tikam reported that a female cousin had thrown up in the bathroom. She had then elaborately described to everyone the circumstances that led to her vomiting: the sight of leftover rice, tangled in masses of hair, floating near the open drain. Rajiv was determined no one, least of all Niveeta, should tell more tales about the dubious standards of hygiene his household maintained, so he started cleaning. He looked around the kitchen and sighed at how filthy it was.

The area around the electrical wiring above the stove was black with grime, and the lone kitchen lightbulb, unchanged for years, hung nearly opaque with dirt. He thought of discarding it but opted instead to scrape off the greasy residue with a knife. It took a long time, but when he plugged the bulb back in after washing and drying it, the light shone with an intensity that forced him to squint. A giant spider crawled up his arm as he knocked loose the cobwebs that dangled everywhere from the tin roof. On seeing that Tikam had done an unsatisfactory job doing the morning dishes,

Rajiv washed them again. He stopped only when his grandmother expressed concern that he was working himself to death.

Hardly had the euphoria of this major accomplishment seeped in when he saw the bedroom. The floor, its cracks and pits ignored for decades, would stubbornly cling to its dirt, rendering most of his elbow grease useless. Patching these holes would have to wait until after he found a job. A pile of rusty tin trunks stuffed with clothes threatened to tumble over. Rajiv started with the bedsheets and mattresses, under which lay mismatched socks. Two roaches skittered to safety as he stripped the beds. He scrubbed and wrung out months of accumulated saliva, sweat, and dirt from the sheets.

He wouldn't have minded an extra hand, but it was silly to expect his grandmother to be useful. She did what she could by spreading out the clothes he had salvaged from the tin boxes to disinfect in the sun. His brother hadn't made an appearance since leaving early that morning, and Tikam was busy chasing crowing roosters in the front yard, so Rajiv continued his solitary effort. But when he found what was under the beds—yellowed, silverfish-infested books and tattered clothes heaped in a foul-smelling bundle that he was certain housed mouse droppings—he gave up. Overcome by exhaustion and feeling defeated by the impending work, he lay on one of the mattresses on the terrace and fell asleep.

It was almost dark when he awoke. Sandeep walked out from the bathroom, freshly bathed and whistling the tune of an old Bollywood song. Rajiv's head throbbed, and he asked Sandeep if he'd get him some water. Sandeep called for Tikam but received no answer.

"He's never here when you need him," his brother grumbled, going to the kitchen. "I have to do all the work around here."

The water he handed Rajiv was cold. With every gulp, Rajiv pushed down an entire day's worth of pent-up anger.

"You know I don't drink cold water," he said.

Sandeep pretended not to hear. Rajiv looked at the glass and then at Sandeep, who was clearly trying to avoid his gaze.

Certain that his brother wouldn't answer, Rajiv left for the bathroom. He filled the plastic bucket to the brim with water and took off his clothes. When he reached for his Lifebuoy soap (after being inspired by a particularly enlightening talk on hygiene with the Scotts, he had just two weeks ago declared to everyone at home that he would use a separate soap that no one was to touch), he saw on it a helix of hair. On the other side of the soap were several strands of hair of varying lengths. He tried removing the hairs with his fingers, but they obstinately remained. His nails dug into the soap, turning pink.

The anger came back in flashes. Several emotions surged in turns, each trying to subdue another but managing only to compound it. He thought of the day he'd had—his uncle's sudden appearance, his grandmother's jabs for not finding a job soon, and his brother's lack of consideration—and confirmed what he had little doubt about: he received zero appreciation from his family. They took all his sacrifices for granted. Not one soul, not even Tikam, whose workload Rajiv tried to lighten in every possible way so he could concentrate on school, had said a nice word to him all day.

Lifting a bucket of ice-cold water and pouring it over himself didn't change anything. He stretched—his back still hurt, and every bone in his body smarted—as he heard loud, urgent knocks on the bathroom door. Tikam was calling out his name and beating the door repeatedly. Just a few months ago, after some very careful budgeting and making a few sacrifices, Rajiv had hired workers to break down the wall separating the toilet and the bathroom and replaced the Eastern-style squatter toilet with a commode for his grandmother's convenience. The renovations had gone well, and even his grandmother was happy she didn't have to squat anymore. Because everyone woke up at different hours, the times for bathroom usage seldom overlapped. At the moment, though, Rajiv concluded that not all was sane about his replacing the two rooms with one. It was, he cursed, a silly, Western thing to do.

He didn't even get a moment's peace in this house. He dressed slowly as the knocks grew more frequent.

"It's almost in my pants," Tikam screamed, first jocularly, then with seriousness.

Rajiv applied some gel to his head and combed his hair. Dissatisfied with the way he looked, he styled his hair again, this time parting it in the middle. He sprayed cologne under his arms.

"Please, please, Dada," Tikam cried.

Rajiv saw he was wearing his T-shirt inside out and took it off to put it back on again. When he opened the door, Tikam was gone. Rajiv was sure Tikam was defecating in some isolated corner of the backyard. When his cousin returned, relieved but with a smell emanating from him that gave away the act he had just committed, Rajiv summoned him.

"Why did you knock when I was in the bathroom?" he asked.

"Dada, it was almost out," Tikam said. "In my pants. One more second, and it would have been on the floor."

"But you knew I was in there."

"And you didn't open the door despite how many times I knocked. A hundred times I knocked."

"What makes you think I'll give up whatever I am doing for you?"

"But I could have dirtied the floor, Dada, and you didn't open the door."

"This is my house, and I'll spend however long it takes me in the bathroom, get it?" Rajiv's voice rose. "From now on, if you ever knock when I am in the bathroom, I'll stop sending you to school and increase the chores you do here."

He boxed Tikam's ears and then slapped him hard on the face. He pulled his hair. Tikam's sobs grew louder as the beating progressed to kicking. Tikam was now on all fours. The kicks were aimed at the shins, the stomach and the head. By the time Rajiv was done, the neighbors on Zakir Hussain Road were all out of their houses. Curious tourists from Andy's Guest House peeped out to confirm their horror. Rajiv felt liberated by the animal inside him he had unleashed.

"Just because we are related doesn't mean you can take advantage of me, Tikam," he spat. "You will never, never, never knock on the door again when I'm in the bathroom."

Finally at peace with himself for a reason he didn't quite understand, he pushed Tikam away.

The Scotts arrived right on time the next morning. In their hands, they each held a copy of the New Testament.

"How was Sunday?" Christa said.

Rajiv told them all. He started with his *mama*, his grandmother's insults, the backbreaking cleaning, and the beating.

"Do you regret it?" Michael asked.

"Regret what?"

"Beating Tikam for no fault of his."

"I don't," Rajiv said. "It felt good."

"Can you elaborate for us, Rajiv?" Michael asked. If he condemned Rajiv's actions or justification, he let neither his tone nor expression reveal it.

"I don't know, Mr. Scott, it was a long day, and when I beat him, I felt less like a victim. The more he screamed in pain, the less my pain became, the less I felt like I was suffering."

"Do you think it was a contest thing?" Michael said.

"Contest?" Rajiv was confused.

"Yes, a competition, as in his sufferings should be more than yours."

"I didn't look at it that way," Rajiv confided.

Tikam walked to them bearing three glasses of tea. His eyes were still swollen from crying. No physical hurt was evident, but he refused to look up when Michael cheerfully greeted him.

"The sight of him—doesn't it break your heart?" Michael asked as Tikam turned around.

"I don't know." Rajiv took a sip of his tea and grimaced at its bitterness. "No, it doesn't. It's twisted, but I'll say it—I think he deserved it."

"We aren't here to preach, but violence isn't the answer, Rajiv," Christa said.

"Is that what the New Testament says?"

"No, it's not only what the Bible says," replied Christa. "It's something every religion in the world teaches."

She spoke more slowly than she usually did and enunciated every word. Christa was definitely more transparent than Michael—she was letting her disapproval show.

"You don't know about all religions," Rajiv testily declared. He was surprised he was talking to the Scotts that way. "Just today a court in the UAE declared that it wasn't anti-Islamic for a man to use violence on his wife or children."

"It doesn't make it right, Rajiv," Christa said. She had stopped sipping her tea.

"I didn't say it's right, Ms. Scott." Rajiv let go of the handle of his cup and gripped it by the body. "I just find it weird that you claim to know all religions."

"This isn't about religion at all, Rajiv," Christa said. "I am afraid—"

Before she could finish, Michael said, "Are you ashamed of your poverty, Rajiv?"

"Who said I am poor, Mr. Scott?"

"No, no one said that, but I think you're stressed about your relatives' arrival. It's festival time; you should try to enjoy yourself. Too much attention to their needs is making the holidays painful for you. You must remember you can still eat and have a roof above your head—that's more than what many people in this country have."

"But you have to understand I have a lot of people visiting," Rajiv said. "And they aren't here to see Sandeep or me but to feel better about themselves, to use us to teach their children that they need to be grateful for their good fortune. I know they'll gossip about our one-bedroom house all the way back to Shillong. If they came here with nobler intentions, maybe I'd look forward to their visit."

"Why do you let their pettiness bother you?" Michael asked. "You're worrying endlessly about what they think. Aren't you giving them the power to control you? Why is what they think so important to you?"

"It's easy for you to say all that, Mr. Scott, but these people bought me my engineering degree. My mother's sisters and brothers—the four of them—each paid for a year of my college. They expect me to be obligated to them even though I have already paid them all in full after our Kurseong property was sold to those hotel developers last year. I wanted to pay them a little interest, so I wouldn't have to feel indebted for life, but that's not done with your close relatives."

"They helped you in times of need, Rajiv." The aggressive tone in Christa's voice disappeared. "Shouldn't you be thankful to them?"

"If thanks were all that was needed, it would be okay. I can't stand their patronizing attitude. Even their children know I wouldn't have gone to engineering college had it not been for their parents. It's in the way they treat me, in the way they treat Sandeep."

"You just have to see them once a year, Rajiv," Michael said.

"My *mama* is the worst of all, Mr. Scott, and he lives in Darjeeling."

"But you rarely see him," Christa reminded him. "You're thinking of these people so much that you're venting out your frustrations on others—it was Tikam yesterday, and it's me today. If it's just twice a year that you see him, that's not a problem."

"And when I do see him, I have to make sure Tikam is far away so I don't take out all my anger on him," Rajiv said.

Before they left, Christa gave Rajiv a copy of the New Testament and told him to read it. It was, she said, the best way to understand Christianity. They weren't trying to convert him, she added. For someone who was losing faith in everything around him, reaffirming his faith in God—any god—might do a lot of good. They were, of course, available anytime he wanted to discuss the book. There was one for his brother, too, but Michael suggested it'd be a better idea to ask Sandeep first before assuming he was going to read a book—any book.

Feeling partly guilty about having been rude to Christa, Rajiv set about cleaning again. Sandeep was still sleeping, and Rajiv didn't wake him up. His grandmother was rotating the knob of her radio to pick up signals from All India Radio Kurseong. He hadn't seen Tikam since he'd brought them tea that morning. Rajiv took a blouse—it probably belonged to his mother—from under his bed and wiped the windows and frames with it. When he removed the pictures from where they were positioned on the walls to wipe their backs, more displaced silverfish hurried about. He killed one or two and let the others live. The dust that had gathered on the pictures provoked his allergies, and he wrapped another of his mother's blouses around his nose and mouth. When the coughing wouldn't stop, he headed to the terrace, where his grandmother advised him to look up to the sky as soon as he felt the coughs coming. It miraculously worked.

As his grandmother muttered details of a few old wives' tales, Rajiv washed the *khadas* that adorned the picture frames.

He'd have thrown them away and not replaced them with new ones, but the pictures by themselves looked incomplete. The people in them looked alive without the *khadas* around them. To Rajiv, that was wrong. He stared at his father's photo and felt an eerie sense of bonding—he looked exactly like his father. He tried to stir up an emotion from his mother's photo and failed. He stared the longest at his grandfather's face, wiped the frame once again, and put the picture back where it belonged. He'd have to make sure the *khadas* looked brand new.

In the evening, he tackled the mess beneath the beds. To add color to the drab room, he rescued the books from under the beds and placed them on the windowsill. He had gone to St. Paul's, a Christian school that, impressed with his academic brilliance, had taken him in for no fee. The beginning of each academic session, in late February, his father helped cover all his and Sandeep's books with brown paper; sometimes Appa stapled a transparent plastic sheet over the covering.

As a child, Rajiv loved writing his name on the book covers with an irregular mixture of upper- and lowercase letters. Sandeep, never academically inclined, begged his parents for leftover paper so he could construct little planes, which tore at an alarming frequency. Now, unable to resist leafing through the same moth-eaten books—big sections of Rajiv's were meticulously underlined and full of side notes, while Sandeep's were clean and barely used—he was transported to simpler, happier times. He didn't remember his relatives treating him shoddily then. He didn't remember a single responsibility. Except a few times, like when they beat him because he returned Niveeta's bite with a kick, his parents had given him a happy, even spoiled, childhood. His thoughts diverted once again to the biting incident, and he smiled. It would be interesting to remind Niveeta.

* * *

The Scotts surprisingly didn't come the next day. Rajiv, although desperate to talk to them about the positive energy that going through the old books infused him with, was half hoping they wouldn't show up because of the anxiety attack the presence of someone of their faith on a day as holy as the *Tika* might give his grandmother. It was the main event of the ten-day-long *Dashain* festival. On this day, Hindu Nepalis from the neighborhood came to his place to accept *tika*—rice blended with a yogurt-based pink paste—from his grandmother. Everyone, even Sandeep, wore new clothes. Rajiv, for his part, wore a rarely seen button-down shirt he was sure everyone thought was new. His grandmother wore a less sedate sari. Tikam had taken a few days off to visit his family in Teesta. He simply nodded sideways at Rajiv as a gesture of good-bye.

When Rajiv said it was appropriate for her to wear a small red dot on her forehead, his grandmother looked astounded but happy.

"What will people say?" She smiled.

"Why do you care?" Rajiv asked. "Everyone is doing it these days."

"They aren't widows like me."

"Even the widows are doing it."

"I am almost eighty and don't even wear white fully. People might talk."

"I have seen widows as old as you wear pink saris. Your green is decent. I guarantee no one will say a word about your red dot."

"You don't know how women talk." She shushed him.

He didn't pressure her more. He wanted her to know that he understood her desires, and she seemed appreciative, which was all that mattered.

His grandmother smeared the rice blend on her grandsons' foreheads and, as the day progressed, on the neighbors' with

alacrity and happily dispensed blessings. She wasn't familiar
with the standard incantations that went along with the offering
of the *tika*, but Rajiv had recorded two chants—one for males
and the other for females—on his phone, which pleased the
old woman. Most of her immediate family was dead, and Rajiv
was thankful that all these neighbors made her feel elderly and
respected on this day. Almost all of them came bearing plastic
bags full of fruit or boxes of sweetmeat; many even made mon-
etary offerings to her, which his grandmother shyly accepted.
She procured five-rupee notes from under her bra strap as gifts
for the little ones. She beamed when youngsters touched her
feet with their heads.

Dashain also meant feasting. It had become a yearly ritual
with Tamang Uncle, their next-door neighbor, to buy a live
goat, kill it, sacrifice its head at his home altar, and cook the rest
of it in different ways—stewed, barbecued, and fried. His boys
served in the Indian Army and weren't home in October, so
Rajiv, Sandeep, and their grandmother ate more meat at Tamang
Uncle's during *Dashain* than they did the entire year at their
place. They didn't cook anything different from their everyday meals at home during the festival, and Rajiv was glad the
neighbors didn't say anything disparaging because they knew
no one in the house was qualified to prepare a feast. Besides, all
the neighbors were already stuffed with meat by the time they
arrived at Rajiv's place. Some even came drunk.

This year, one fewer family accepted *tika* at their place. Subba
Uncle, who lived two doors down, had converted to Christianity earlier that month. All the five members of the family were
baptized, got rid of their old names, and adopted anglicized
names: Jasraj Subba was now Joseph Subba, while Jamuna, his
wife, was now Jemina. Jasraj had given up alcohol completely,
and Jamuna, a compulsive gambler, stayed away from cards and

the women who played them. Naturally, this invited the ridicule of the neighborhood. The new converts were active in their church and their grown-up daughters were already training to become Sunday School teachers.

Rajiv had a strong suspicion the Scotts had something to do with this change of faith and made a mental note to ask them about it the next day. He then remembered his outburst at Christa and immediately felt ashamed of himself. The Scotts had been nice to him and had taught him to see the world from a different perspective than he was wont to do, and his behavior with Christa—who had been pretty civil despite everything—was uncalled for. He knew, though, that he would never get around to reading the New Testament. It wasn't because he was a die-hard Hindu; he just didn't attribute enough importance to religion to want to change from the one he was born into.

As light gave way to dark, and the last of the revelers left, Rajiv's apprehension returned. He'd have to wake up again in the morning and give the corners a thorough sweep. His grandmother was already snoring, and Sandeep was out with friends. Rajiv knew he should have gone to his *mama*'s place for *tika*, but he was certain his uncle, true to form, would ruin this nice day in some way or the other. He wondered if he'd invite his *mama*'s wrath the next day or if his wealthy uncle barely noticed the absence of his nephew.

Mama's call woke him up the next day.

"Still asleep," the other man said. "I thought so. Were you up all night drinking?"

"I don't drink, *Mama*," Rajiv said.

"I don't believe you."

"Do you know what time Manju *chema* will get here?"

"I am not their attendant. Just don't disappear to your *adda* during the day. Be sure you are home when they arrive. They could come anytime. Their cell is still out of range."

"Can you give the number to me?" Rajiv asked. He thought he could keep trying until he reached them to ask what time they'd be there.

His uncle had disconnected the phone already, which Rajiv wasn't surprised about. Abruptly hanging up without saying good-bye was a common trait among all his mother's relatives. They had done it every time they called him regarding some fee-related issue in college.

He called out to his grandma. She didn't hear him. His brother's bed was empty. He probably hadn't come home last night.

When the Scotts arrived and he made them tea, he wondered if he should offer them fruit or sweetmeat from the day before. Christians he knew from Darjeeling usually didn't eat anything that was first offered to Hindu gods.

"Would you also like some guavas and *burfee*?" Rajiv asked.

"Wow! Guavas would be very nice," Christa exclaimed while Michael nodded in agreement.

"They came as *parshads*. Is that okay?"

"Absolutely," Christa said.

Rajiv thought they might not have understood what *parshads* were.

"*Parshads* are offerings made to Hindu gods."

"Why shouldn't we eat them?" Michael looked puzzled.

Rajiv hastened to explain. "No, Christians in Darjeeling don't eat them."

"Nothing comes between me and my guavas," Christa said, as she bit a ripe one. "Delicious. And we are different Christians."

"So when do they arrive?" Michael asked, referring to the guests.

"Sometime today."

"All cousins?" inquired Christa.

"No, an aunt, a cousin, and the cousin's cousin."

"Ooooh, the cousin's cousin is not related to you, right?" It was Christa again.

"No, she's not," Rajiv said uncomfortably.

"Have you ever met her?" Christa asked.

"Yes, once."

He told them about the biting episode. They all laughed.

"Quite the enigmatic person this cousin's cousin is," Christa teased. "Childhood bites and all."

"What's an enigma is the Subba family," Rajiv said.

"Why?" Christa and Michael said in unison.

"Didn't they convert?"

"Oh, yes, they've accepted the Lord as their savior," Christa said, her eyes lighting up.

"Were you sort of responsible for it?" Rajiv asked.

"We helped them accept Christ," Christa said. "We wouldn't call ourselves responsible for their conversion. We were merely agents along the way."

Rajiv looked at Michael, expecting him to say something. Michael kept quiet.

"Why do you do it?" Rajiv asked.

"Do what?" Michael finally said.

"You know—convert people."

"Have we tried converting you?" Christa asked.

"Not really, although you did ask me to read the Bible."

"We also prefaced the Bible-reading request with a no-conversion-intention guarantee," said Christa.

"Okay," Rajiv said. "But why do you convert people? What's in it for you?"

"You make it sound like we kill people," Christa said. She was flustered.

Michael was calm. Rajiv knew he would never see Michael lose his cool.

"You do kill people's faith in the religion they were born into."

"People aren't born into a religion." Christa was shifty.

"But you still haven't told me why you do it."

"What's your favorite movie?" Christa asked.

"It's a Bollywood one."

"All right, did you insist all your friends watch it?" she continued.

"Yes, I wanted them all to watch it."

"Your favorite book?"

"I like *The Alchemist*."

"Did you want all your friends to experience the book?"

"Yes, I did."

Michael took over. "Christianity makes us happy. We want our friends, all the people we meet, to experience what we experience. It's like you want your friend to watch a movie that made you happy so he can become happy, too."

This was the first time Michael had openly talked about Christianity. He looked so content.

"That's a ridiculous reason." Rajiv laughed bitterly. "You think I am so glib."

"We think you are being disrespectful, Rajiv," Christa said. "You haven't been yourself since the news of your relatives' arrival."

"Yes, and probably reading the Bible will help make me better, right, Christa?" It was the first time he had called her that.

"It's easy to transfer your anger from them to us, from family to religion, Rajiv," Christa said, slightly tearful and looking to Michael for support. "I think we should talk next when you're back to your senses."

"That's a good idea," Rajiv said, with mock respect. "Raju next door will be easier to convert than me. And please continue eating the *parshad*. You're different from other Christians after all."

The Scotts put down their *burfees* and walked out. Michael gave Rajiv a look he had often seen on his *mama's* face—that of pure, undisguised disgust.

But Rajiv had little time to worry about that. Niveeta and her party would arrive soon. He shopped for groceries, checked that the floors were not sticky, organized the books on the sill in a variety of arrangements, and readjusted the crumpled sheets on whichever bed his grandmother lay. Intermittently, he thought about what happened with the Scotts and wondered if he'd ever see them again. He wasn't going to apologize to them. His father had been right all along. Rajiv wouldn't let them bother him— thankfully, Niveeta's presence was enough to make him temporarily block the Scotts from his mind.

She looked just like his cousin Sona—both were about twenty-one and had the same big eyes uncommon among Rais, three moles on the right cheek and a complexion the color of chalk. Niveeta was slightly taller than Sona, but otherwise they were mirror images of each other. In fact, Rajiv was sure people mistook them for twins. He was so taken aback by the similarity between his cousin and his cousin's cousin that he couldn't help himself from looking at them over and over again, which Niveeta caught him doing several times.

Rajiv wheeled their suitcases into the bedroom, all the while hoping they wouldn't ask where the sitting room was. An aunt had once made the mistake of inquiring about the sitting room, and Rajiv hadn't known how to answer. She understood his jumpy silence and didn't pursue the matter further, but Rajiv, to this day, remembered the humiliation he suffered at the insensitive query. But again, he was sure these people wouldn't ask him embarrassing questions because the aunt had probably already briefed them on what his house looked like and which topics to avoid.

"The three of you could have a bed each with Boju in this room, and I'll sleep in the next room," he said.

He hoped they wouldn't ask him what the next room was.

"Can I sleep in the next room instead?" Niveeta asked. "I am habituated to sleeping alone."

"You'd have to sleep on the floor." Rajiv rubbed his left shoe against his right shin.

"I don't mind the floor as long as I am alone in the room," Niveeta said.

Rajiv looked at his aunt for help. She was carefully studying the uneven ceiling and the shelf of books.

"There are cockroaches on the floor," he said.

"Psst, like I care about them," Niveeta said.

Finally, realizing he had no other way out, he said it: "The other room is the kitchen."

Three incredulous pairs of eyes stared at him.

"Let me go get you some tea," Rajiv said, excusing himself.

On his return with three glasses of tea, the threesome halted their conversation.

"This tea is delicious," Niveeta said.

"Delicious," his aunt echoed.

It was overcompensating. Fortunately, his grandmother was out at some neighbor's.

"Because she can't sleep by herself in the kitchen, we've decided to book a room at Andy's Guest House next door," his aunt said nonchalantly. "It will be close to here, and we won't disturb your grandmother's sleep."

"But you don't have to," Rajiv spluttered. "I could move her bed into the kitchen."

"No, don't worry about it," Sona said. "We'll just stay at Andy's. They have a bucketful of hot water per person in the morning. We stayed there during our school trip last year."

And she didn't even call me to let me know she was in town, thought Rajiv. The fool didn't even know she just blabbered something she shouldn't have said.

"She was in a school group, and no one was allowed to contact relatives," her mother instantly said.

It was a feeble lie.

"Shouldn't we at least call them first?" Sona asked.

She did, and was told the guest house had one last room left.

"Some Spanish girls canceled at the last minute because one of them was too sick to leave Delhi today," she said with a laugh.

"Let's go, then," Niveeta said.

"Will you be back for dinner?"

Rajiv had shopped for *paneer* and *kinema* earlier in the day and had even asked Sandeep to come home early to help with the cooking.

"We need to go put on *tika* at *mama*'s," Sona said. "We might just eat there. That's where everyone is."

With great effort, he dragged their suitcases through the terrace, carried them down the stairs, wheeled them up the road and lugged them up the staircase at Andy's. No one helped him. When they checked in, no one bothered thanking him for getting a hundred-rupee discount, offered to those the owner at Andy's knew.

His aunt booked just one room, nullifying Niveeta's claim that she couldn't sleep unless she was alone. Niveeta sat down on one of the beds in their room, exclaiming with delight at the quaintness of the guest house. Rajiv shot her a look. She saw him look at her and subconsciously ran her hand over her side and back to see if her underwear band showed. She pulled her

T-shirt down a bit, pulled up her pants slightly and brought her hand to her hair.

Rajiv told his aunt he was leaving. She handed him a 500-rupee note for *Dashain*, but Rajiv wouldn't accept it despite how unyielding she was.

His grandmother was slowly negotiating the stairs to their place when he returned home. She was wondering where the guests were.

"They were stuck in Guwahati," he said. "They might just head back home instead."

"Silly people—your mother's family," she said.

"I think I'll go to bed early today," said Rajiv.

"Also, Tikam called," his grandmother said. "He won't be coming back. He says he'll stay home and learn farming."

"I'll go to sleep. Have Sandeep cook you something."

"He's not coming home, I am sure," she said, leaving the room. "Just my luck to starve to death the day after *Tika*."

He stared at Tikam's empty bed, put out the light, and lay down. He wondered what might transpire at *mama*'s place tonight. Would they all be horrified at the idea of Niveeta's sleeping in the kitchen? He speculated about what the Scotts would have said. He thought of what his father would have done in a situation like this, what his mother would have had to say at the end of the day. Through the dark, he looked at where his parents' pictures hung, saw their faces in his mind's eye, and said a prayer over and over again. It was a Christian prayer he had been taught at St. Paul's.

No Land Is Her Land

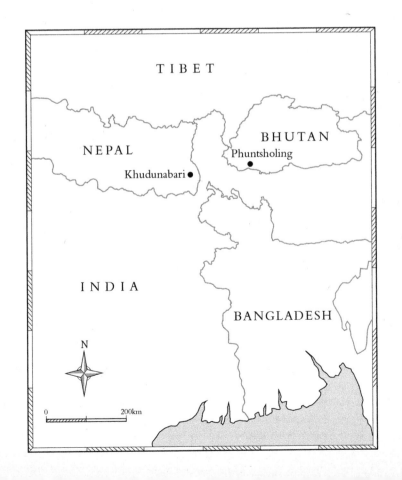

Anamika Chettri kicked off the tendrils that stubbornly clung to her feet as she stopped every fifty meters along the dirt trail to collect kindling. With the kerosene ration halved in the refugee camps and the coal briquettes aggravating her aging father's cough, the sticks available outside her camp in Khudunabari appeared to be her best option. Some of her neighbors said her father probably had TB and that Anamika should ask a camp doctor to have a look at him—a suggestion she paid no heed to, for she had too many things to worry about. There was no telling, anyway, what further problems a diagnosis would unravel.

Anamika rolled up her summer shawl, placed it on her head as a cushion and balanced the heavy bundle of wood on it before hiking down the trail with a tightrope walker's gait.

The college men were at the *singara* shop, their usual spot. Anamika's pace quickened. She steeled herself for what was to come by saying a silent prayer to God and mentally rehearsing suitable comebacks. Fear wouldn't paralyze her tongue the way it did many years ago. She had become adept at giving back the men what they deserved.

"*Wah*," one of the four exclaimed. "Look at her walk—she goes swish, swish, swish, swish."

"Her hips swing like the clock's pendulum." It was the long-haired rascal whom she had slapped in public last month.

"Is that why you keep staring at them?" Anamika snapped without looking back. "To tell the time? Because you can't read the clock, you illiterate fool?"

"Go back to your damn country." Another voice, shriller than the rest, brought applause and hoots from the crew. "Go to Bhutan. No one wants you in Nepal."

"Wait, I want her here. I want her all to myself."

"Yes, shake your *condo* back to Bhutan. We don't need the likes of you to torture us with your looks here."

"Stop bothering me, you mangy dogs." A twig from her bundle fell. "Go back to your mothers and wives, but they are too busy dancing with the Maoists, aren't they?"

"*Lyaa*, Lutey, she called your wife a whore," shouted the man she slapped. "It can't be my wife. I have no wife."

"A whore calling a decent woman a whore." Peals of laughter.

"She's thirty-five and has the mouth of a fifteen-year-old bitch. Who would think of a mother having such a filthy tongue? Her older daughter must have picked up all the good words by now. She looks just like her."

"Yes, she looks just like me, and she's more of a man than you all will ever be." The retorts today were better and faster than last week's.

"She looks so young—how can she have children?"

"Want me to show it to you?" Loud moans followed while Anamika tried to keep her face wooden.

"There are two of them."

"No, three."

"No, five."

"She's a factory, a baby factory." Loud laughter.

"Yes, except she likes changing the raw material to make babies with. Different fathers for different babies."

"I learned that from your mother, *kukkur*," she shouted.

She was inured to it all, hardly enraged. It was almost over. She had already turned the corner and was out of sight.

Anamika ran home, stopping only when she reached her hut and hurled the bundle in one corner. Her father was sleeping. At his feet, her daughters were writing Dzongkha letters on a notebook-sized blackboard—the camp school had recently introduced Dzongkha studies in hopes that the children wouldn't find the repatriation process so difficult when Bhutan eventually allowed them in. Her neighbors, who lived in the adjoining hut and shared the outhouse with them, were slicing, dicing, pickling, and bottling raw mangoes behind the kitchen. The skies were overcast; she'd have to bring the clothes in before the rains came.

Anamika considered the refugee camp at Khudunabari her home. She wasn't the kind to stare into the open space and sigh longingly for Bhutan. Her theory was simple: if her country (she still referred to Bhutan as her country even after all these years) didn't want her, she didn't want it back. She had long ago learned to let go—of the eight acres of land her family owned close to Phuntsholing, of the cousins left behind who scraped through the citizenship test that, thanks to her husband, she had failed, and of the food, anointed with copious amounts of cheese and hot peppers, that she had never quite succeeded in replicating since she came to Nepal as one of the 106,000 ethnic-Nepalese refugees forced out of Bhutan.

Khudunabari wasn't all that different from Phuntsholing. The people looked alike, spoke Nepali with the expected variance in inflection, and followed the same religion and customs. The Bhutanese refugees at the camps often declared that they had done a better job of preserving the Nepalese culture than the Nepalese people themselves. Despite living in such familiar

surroundings, most refugees she spoke to were hoping for repatriation, unlike Anamika. She had had it with Bhutan. Her
daughter's repetition of Dzongkha letters should have brought
back memories, but it didn't. It was as though the girl were par-
roting English nursery rhymes, nothing more. Anamika felt no
stirrings in her heart, as the camp folks often claimed, no senti-
ment for a country that was once her home.

"What did you learn at school today?" she asked neither of
the girls in particular. Anamika had studied up to eighth grade
in Phuntsholing.

"What would you understand, Aamaa?" Shambhavi, the
ten-year-old, whispered. She could have shouted. Anamika's
father could sleep through anything—even the agitation in
Bhutan.

"I am not uneducated like our neighbors, Shambhavi, and
you'll get a slap for talking back to me that way."

"We talked about settling in some foreign country."

"What do you mean?"

"Don't you know?" twelve-year-old Diki asked, shifting positions to avoid being hit by drops of water trickling through the
roof.

Anamika asked her to place a bucket where the water had
formed a small puddle on the mud floor. Some stray drops
landed on the sleeping old man's toes and made the girls giggle.

"The America story? It's been going on since we first arrived
here. At your age you believe everything they say, Diki."

"But they say it's true this time," Diki said. "America will take
some of us."

"Even if it is true, how do they choose who goes and who
doesn't?" Anamika asked with a dismissive hand motion. "And
what about those left behind?"

"They said in class that America would take those who are
fit, not very old, and can speak English," said Diki.

"Speak English?" Anamika said. "That means almost all of us cannot go."

"But the teacher said we shouldn't talk about it too much," Diki continued. "Some people do not like the idea of America taking us. They think that will make Bhutan happy, and they don't want Bhutan happy."

"They've been talking about it for seventeen years, long before I came here," said Anamika as she rubbed a handful of ash at the bottom of a burned pot and ran water over it. "One day it was London, and the next day it was Australia. I've stopped believing it."

"Will we still get rations in America, Aamaa?" Shambhavi asked.

"Probably."

"And will Baajey join us if we get to go? He is not young, not fit, and barely knows an English word."

"If I knew all the answers, wouldn't I be God? Now go back to your studies. You take every opportunity to waste your time."

Anamika had wasted a dozen years of her life at the camp. Back in Bhutan, she had at least been working, contributing to her family. Even after her marriage, she regularly deposited small amounts of money into her father's new Bank of Bhutan account. Her husband probably didn't notice because he was too busy enticing every Nepali-speaking Bhutanese within reach to join the revolution. For her husband, the passion for the cause of the ethnic Nepalese in Bhutan came belatedly—years after the Bhutanese government had silenced the first murmurs of dissent. He had changed in a short time, not in his behavior toward her, for he was still affectionate, but in the way he interacted with people around him. He was constantly organizing, had little by little cut off the few non-Nepali-speaking Bhutanese acquaintances from his life and stopped working altogether.

Their dream of starting their own business in partnership with an Indian Marwari from Jaigaon was just taking shape—the hardware store would technically be theirs, for the Marwari couldn't acquire a license as a foreigner in Bhutan. He'd run it, and they'd learn as much as they could while sharing the profits before finally going at another venture alone. Anamika would resign from her government job in a few weeks while her husband carried on working until the enterprise generated a profit. It had all been perfectly mapped out.

But the business planning halted, and her husband stopped going to his job as a typist in the court at Phuntsholing. If the new people's hero did show up at work, it was at odd hours, brandishing an antimonarchy pamphlet and dressed in *daura suruwal*, the Nepali costume for men, despite the Bhutanese government's having just mandated that only traditional Bhutanese attire be worn at offices. From a belt around his waist dangled a sheathed *khukuri*, the curved Nepalese knife, with his hand often resting on the wooden handle. Half a dozen men, most of whom dressed like him, always accompanied her husband.

Anamika returned home from work one day to discuss whether it was wise to quit her job the next week, as had been planned, when issues like job security and money were still important to her husband. Things weren't the same as before, what with her husband's not working, and she wanted to be sure before she took so dramatic a step.

"Why quit?" he absentmindedly said without looking up from the back of a calendar, on which he was scribbling notes. "It's our government also. Or have you begun believing them when they say we don't belong here? We may be ethnic Nepali, but we are Bhutanese, too."

"What about starting the store? We need time. I need to learn."

"Tell me if that's good." He threw a carefully coined slogan at her. "We are humans, not animals. We should be allowed to speak our language, not bark yours."

He said it with a singsong cadence, repeated it and found something amiss.

"No, no, that didn't come out right. Let's try this: 'One people, one country' doesn't work when we are made to feel like the others."

"They have finally stopped throwing people out by the truckloads near the borders." Anamika wanted to tear his notebook. "They may start again because of your demonstrations. Should we risk being let out?"

"The king—the king has to go. We are Bhutanese, too, so what if we are a little different from the majority of you?"

"The store, what about the store?" Anamika asked, aware she had slipped into the same lilt as he did with his slogans.

"The king, the king, out with the king," he sang. "A democracy is what we need."

Pleased, he wrote it down.

"Wait, this one is slightly better. The king, the king, out with the king. A democracy is the need of the hour."

"Do you want something to eat?" She was exhausted.

"Ethnicity, ethnicity," he shouted. "We're being kicked out for no other reason than our ethnicity."

"Should I serve you food?"

She hadn't cooked anything. Neither had he.

"Do away with 1958. Some of us can show you the documents while others, we cannot." He was referring to the 1958 citizenship documents the government required all Nepali-speaking people residing in the country to procure as proof of their citizenship. "We have papers from 1957, we have papers from 1959. But to you, merciless king, none but 1958 will do. Thoo, thoo, thoo," he venomously spat out three times.

*   *   *

Anamika soon found out that Diki's talk about resettlement hadn't been entirely incorrect. The camp was abuzz with excitement about the recent developments. Everyone knew scraps of information, but no one had the details.

Yes, America was settling sixty thousand of them in her states. No force was used. Yes, everyone knew someone who knew someone an American had already interviewed at the International Organization for Migration office in Damak. Someone said every family would have a separate bathroom—sometimes, even two bathrooms—and no one would go hungry. America would also give them jobs and teach them English. It would be difficult to teach the old ones, so America didn't like them so much. Maybe America would use the young ones to fight the Muslims, a neighbor pointed out. Thankfully, America disliked Muslims but liked Hindus and Buddhists the best.

The interviews would take place in the same red air-conditioned building where the blood tests would be done. Yes, the women wore pants, and only pants, in America, and the men weren't allowed to lay hands on women. They could still beat up the wives secretly, but the wives could always inform the police. No, no, no, another know-it-all said, don't try your "sir/madam" *chamchagiri*; the Americans saw right through you when you tried to flatter them, because they went to school to gauge that. Yes, England might take some. And maybe Australia and Norway, too.

Anamika believed that all these years of promises might come to something real when she saw buses just outside the camp one rainy day. These weren't the ailing vehicles she saw around Khudunabari. They looked brand new. Close by, a group of bystanders was involved in a heated discussion—the Nepalese from outside the camp, among them the shrill-voiced *singara* shop regular, told stories that contradicted what had been discussed at the camp.

"Is America everyone's orphanage that it will take their lot?" the man from the *singara* shop said to the others milling around him.

"Yes, it will," Anamika said. "They see how we live because of constant harassment from animals like you."

"*Loo hera*," he said. "We offer them shelter, and instead of gratitude, we receive those words."

"You deserve worse," came the reply from an old lady, a camp neighbor, who sat on the ground and lit her *beedi*.

"Now the old woman has courage, too." The man's voice was even shriller; it could have been a woman's voice. "This Anamika *aaimaai* is teaching everyone to talk back to us. Women talk like men. Men are afraid of women. What has the world come to?"

"If you talk like that, I'll slap you like I slapped your friend."

"Will some of you marry us if they allow you to go to America?" His face softened.

"We would get married to these dogs around here before to you useless fools." Anamika threw a pebble at a pair of mating dogs, which obediently decoupled, and, still in heat, scampered to another pack nearby.

"It's unfair that you should get to go while we don't." He looked wistful, almost sad.

"You are a married man." It was the first time Anamika was having a real conversation with him. "What nonsense are you talking about getting married to one of us? That fat wife of yours needs to keep you under lock and key every day."

"You can marry me, Anamika." He looked serious. "What's a third husband when you've already had two?"

"I plan on taking seven husbands, but they will be real men—not women like you. Have you even heard your own voice? It's like your mother forced cat's milk down your throat when you were a baby."

The old woman laughed loudly, inciting Anamika to carry on.

"You know how to deal with them," the woman said. "I am sure Lord Brahma regrets having given life to these men."

"I am sure their mothers regret having given birth to them," Anamika added, and lest she should get enraged and cause physical harm to the offending man, she, too, sat down beside the woman. "Where are these buses taking our people?"

"They're going for interviews," the woman said.

"Interviews? Shouldn't we go, then?"

The people on the first bus cheered when the engine revved.

"No, they only select some people. My children's father says it will be a long process. It has already taken more than Ram's *ban-baas*."

"What about the rest of us?"

"Some of us they won't take."

"What are the criteria?"

The second bus honked, and the passengers shouted, "America, America." The driver got off, and the passengers shouted, "No America, no America" amid loud laughter.

"They say America needs soldiers to fight wars, so they will give preference to men—young, able-bodied men. I know God will take care of me because I have sons. They grew up strong despite the lack of meat in this camp."

"I'll probably not get to go then."

"Yes, the camp also keeps track of people's character. Everyone knows of your second marriage."

The bus belched black smoke on Anamika as it barreled down the road. The passengers, like revelers on their way to a picnic, chorused Hindi songs.

Anamika knew the woman meant no ill will. Furthermore, it wasn't as if the woman had spoken an untruth. Anamika herself thought she was a woman of loose morals. No matter how hard she tried to justify her actions, she knew somewhere deep within that she had wronged and would pay a price for it one day. It simply was the *aaimaai*'s business, in the way it was the business of everyone at the camp, to question her moral record.

"You talk like I am the only woman in the world who has been married twice," Anamika said, getting up and walking away.

"But you left both of them," the woman persisted.

"And despite that, I am willing to marry you," the *singara* shop man shouted. "America, America."

The old woman chuckled, which encouraged him further.

"Or maybe I can marry your older daughter. How old is she? Thirteen? She's coming of age."

The more excited he became, the shriller his voice turned.

It had almost been thirteen years since a group of soldiers forced their way into her house in Bhutan and, staring hard at her pregnant belly, demanded to know where her husband was. That year, a number of their neighbors had fled—mostly to the Indian state of Assam. The family three doors down had successfully produced its 1958 citizenship documents and was rumored to be staying. The children, who before had frequently visited Anamika because she gave them generous fistfuls of glucose powder, now came nowhere near her house. Early-morning greetings with the family became less cheerful. The teenagers looked at her when their paths crossed but exchanged few words. They've grown up and no longer like glucose powder, Anamika had tried to convince herself.

Anamika's father possessed the documents, but no one came checking. She had heard stories of rape and murder, of soldiers behaving worse than barbarians. Everyone had. Some said the Bhutanese government, aware of the goings-on in the army, had asked the soldiers not to use violence when escorting the

Nepali-speaking people out of their houses and out of the country. And now while the soldiers scrutinized her body, she feared the worst.

"Whose baby is that?" a soldier asked in Dzongkha.

"My husband's."

"When are you due?" He was gentler now.

"In a month."

"So you saw your husband eight months ago?"

"Yes, I did."

"Was that the last time you saw him?"

"Yes."

"Where are your papers?"

Anamika walked over to the cabinet and showed them photocopies of her father's citizenship card.

"And your husband's?"

It was the question Anamika dreaded.

"It is lost."

"That's convenient."

"But look, my father was here. He even has property documents."

"We aren't concerned with your father. It's your damn husband we care about."

They were moving closer.

Her father, prompted by a neighbor about the soldiers in Anamika's house, arrived at the scene minutes later.

"Did you show the papers?" he asked Anamika.

"Yes, but it's her husband's papers we want."

"You know I don't have those," Anamika said, resigned. "They must be with my husband."

"That's not good enough." The soldier was losing patience. His friends at the door exchanged smirks.

"What now?" Anamika lost her temper. "Will you herd me out of my own country? Like cows and buffaloes?"

"Only those who are law-abiding citizens of this country have the right to live here," he said in Dzongkha.

"You know the line well—is it because you and your soldiers have repeated it more than a hundred thousand times?"

"Only those who are law-abiding citizens of this country have the right to live here," he repeated.

"This is my home, my country." She had to be careful. These soldiers were capable of anything. "I am not going anywhere."

"It is, but it isn't your husband's. He's a criminal."

"Did I know that when I married him?" Anamika cried, quivering with rage. "What if I don't obey your orders? Will you rape me? Why don't you?"

Her father stood silent. For a while, no one spoke.

"Look, sister," a guard finally said in Nepali. "You and I both know what your husband has been up to. We wouldn't like to give you undue stress in your condition, but it would do you good to pack up your necessities. For now, we will pretend we didn't interact with your father. He has the papers, and unfortunately, you don't. You will have to go. The buses will be right there."

Anamika's father wouldn't let his pregnant daughter travel alone. He had the papers, and he could always return if he wanted to. Diki was born at the camp in Nepal. Anamika's father was never allowed back in the country. His son-in-law was a traitor, an enemy of the state. He was a traitor by association.

Anamika was changing when she saw a man with importance scribbled all over his face and sunglasses approach the camp. Her father was the head of this household and the rations were disbursed to him, so she was used to people looking for him. She quickly changed back to the kurta, as draping a sari would take too long, and went out to greet the stranger.

"He's gone out," she said.

"I need to talk to him. It's important. I've come from Damak."

"My daughters aren't here. Otherwise, I'd have sent them out to look for him."

"Can't you go?" he asked.

"There's no one at home."

He looked through the door, as though inspecting just what a thief would steal from the hut. "I could come back some other time, but it's your family's loss. I am a case worker."

"Can you not tell me what it is?"

"No, we need the head of the household."

He meant he needed to talk to someone male.

"You'll have to wait as I shout for him then." Softly, she started, "Baba, Baba."

When a reply wasn't forthcoming, she cupped her hands to her mouth and screamed louder.

Sensing the man's impatience, she asked if he'd like some tea. The man again looked inside, scrutinized the area visible from the door and sulked.

"I'll make you some tea," Anamika repeated. "Please have a seat."

He sat on the jute mat as she blew a fire with a black tin pipe.

"Baba, Baba," she shouted every few seconds.

No sooner did the stranger begin sipping his tea than her father showed up, weighed down by rations.

"*Thet*, squashes," he exclaimed. "They gave them last, and I placed them at the top of my bag. Those thorns kept bothering me throughout."

"Are you the head of the household?" the stranger asked.

"Yes, I am." He looked nervous.

"You've been invited for an interview along with the entire family a week from today. Please report to one of the three buses parked outside at eight in the morning. Do not be late.

This is not Nepal time. The Americans are very particular about punctuality."

"Is this to take us to America?"

"This is just the first interview. I don't have the time to gossip all day. Are there the four of you altogether?"

No one answered.

"And her husband?" He checked the vermilion in the parting of Anamika's hair. "Is he alive?"

"Yes, he is."

"Where is he?"

"Around," her father said.

The man studied Anamika.

"Should all of us come?" Anamika said.

"Didn't I just say that?"

"What should we wear?" her father asked.

"Wear clean clothes."

"What will they ask an old man like me?"

"Nothing that you can lie about."

"We cannot lie?" Anamika said.

"Yes, Americans are very good at spotting lies." His eyes were questioning. "Why? Do you have something to lie about?"

"No, no, I find it unbelievable that they can detect lies."

"They are Americans."

"Will they talk to me in English?" her father asked.

The case worker looked at the father and gave an exasper-ated look to Anamika. He took one final gulp of the tea, saw it was drizzling, asked them if they might have a spare umbrella, smiled to himself at the question and left.

"We'll probably fail," her father said as he crushed tobacco leaves with his trembling hand. "With your marriages and my health, we will fail."

Soon he'd add slaked lime to the fine leaves and pinch the mixture into his mouth, where it would remain safely ensconced between the gum and the lower lip. That her father spat it out anywhere he desired after the tobacco's flavor died infuriated Anamika.

"Why did you keep getting married again and again? You shouldn't have married that good-for-nothing Brahmin. The bastard isn't even here suffering with us when it was his involvement in the demonstrations that got us here in the first place."

He hunted for the container of lime.

"Do you think I'd have married him had I known this would happen?"

He wiped his brow and forehead.

"Okay, but what about the second time? You have no excuse for that. We told you the Karki man was deceptive from the very beginning."

He paused to cough.

"What if they ask me about the marriages? How is it that I have a daughter who brings me so much ill luck?"

"Yes, what if they ask me about the marriages?" Anamika repeated. "We should have asked the case worker, but we didn't, so stay quiet and allow me to think."

Americans are very good at spotting lies, the case worker had said. She'd have to decide what to share and what to eliminate from her story. She knew she had to lie. There was no way the Americans would let a woman like her into their country.

She was beautiful, young, and vulnerable. She had a child whose father was nowhere to be seen. Her father, the only male member in the family, had failing eyesight and could barely hear. She attracted more attention than any other woman at camp. In the beginning, she relished it. It made her feel powerful. Her pride, it soon occurred to her, had been misplaced. It wasn't her beauty that attracted the men as much as it was her helplessness.

The men disliked her because she wasn't their wife, but it was the women who despised her. She was temptation for their husbands, a trap. When she caught somebody's husband spying on her as she washed herself at the communal pump, the consensus at the camp was that it was her fault; it was she who encouraged the man and other husbands. When she confronted the *chutiya*, his wife and a few other wives came together to protect him, called her names, and quizzed her about her absent husband. She realized she had no one to protect her. She'd need a man to guard her, to defend her. And this man wasn't her father.

A Brahmin from outside the camp married her to Ravi Karki, a Nepalese from Birtamod. She'd be Ravi's second wife. The first wife attended the wedding, too. Anamika was asked to summon her as her sister. The first wife had given birth to one daughter after another, and after four daughters, it was understood that Ravi would take another woman. The wedding took place in a temple outside the camp. No one from the camp was invited. Diki would live with her grandfather.

Anamika's new marriage was different from her first. With her eighth-grade education, she was the most schooled person in the family, but that didn't mean she was allowed an opinion. She had to learn to shut up. Ravi's word was the final word. Anamika didn't talk back to him. She had seen Ravi whip the little girls and their mother for no reason. When Ravi beat up the girls, Anamika trained herself to wait for his anger to subside before she talked to him.

Anamika was thankful she was spared the thrashing. If angry at her, Ravi yelled, threatened to hit her, called her a whore, but that was where it ended. Anamika attempted bonding with her "sister," tried to get her to confide in her, but the first wife was distant, as though her husband had specifically asked her not to be friends with Anamika. Her stepdaughters reminded her of Diki, and she often played with them. When Ravi first saw them immersed in hopscotch outside the hut, he asked his new wife if she hadn't anything better to do. That put a stop to the games.

Anamika received her first beating when she dared make a request to Ravi. He had been in a good mood—only one of the girls had received a light spanking.

"I was wondering," Anamika muttered, "if Diki could live with us here."

For a few seconds, Ravi had no idea whom she was talking about. "Who's Diki?"

"My daughter."

"You have no children by me."

The matter would probably have ended there had she not gone on further.

"We already have four daughters in the house. What difference will one more mouth make? I can work myself to feed her if I have to."

To Anamika, it hadn't seemed an outrageous request. She had seen her daughter only once after the marriage five months before.

"I will not have some other man's daughter anywhere near my house," Ravi said, and then, as though struck by lightning, he pounced on her.

"Do you hear that?" He slapped her. He yanked out tufts of her hair. "I already have four useless daughters to feed and clothe because the *randi* is cursed, and you now want me to bring someone else's daughter into this house. I give you a home when you most need it. I marry you when everyone questions your character, and this is how you show your gratitude?"

Then getting up, he kicked her stomach and made a declaration.

"I don't ever want you visiting your daughter or your father. If you do, I promise your daughter will be my third wife once she is old enough."

He then slapped each one of his daughters.

"All you women will destroy me one day," he shouted.

The next morning, he was polite, almost apologetic. That was the last time Anamika ever asked him for anything. The first wife didn't comfort her later that day. The little girls kept stealing glances at Anamika as she massaged her wounds. She contemplated running away, but the thought of a permanent return to the camp was too much to bear. Her father would be mortified. She'd be a woman with no man again, and she didn't want to live through that. It was easier to fear just one man inside the house than to live in constant paranoia of all the men—and women—at the camp.

When Shambhavi was born, Ravi asked Anamika to pack her things.

"I married you so you could give me a son," he gently said. "I can't feed all of you. You and the other *randi* have emasculated me. I have become the laughing stock of the entire neighborhood. I worked hard, I didn't drink, I treated you well, didn't even beat you like I beat her, and what have you given me in return? Yet another burden."

In broad daylight, trying to ignore the whispers and nudges of her neighbors, Anamika, a bundle on her back and a baby in hand, returned to the camp. Her father refused to make eye contact with her. Diki didn't recognize her. Ravi showed up once or twice a year, good-naturedly asked her father for some money and left. He never saw Anamika or his daughter.

The interviews at the International Organization for Migration offices were difficult, everyone said. Just yesterday, a family returned exhausted, the father complaining that they had failed the interview because the American found out they had left Bhutan on their own accord. He could have been lying, but Anamika was nervous.

The white woman wanted all the details. Anamika had problems revisiting them, as she had locked them in the recesses of her mind and hoped she had forever lost the keys to them. Complicating matters was Ravi, who sat there with a forced sullen look on his face, as though he had lived through the harrowing experience himself. He had come into the picture two days ago. News of his wife's good fortune had reached him in no time.

"I've come to see my daughter," he had said. He greeted her father with a Namaste.

"Ten years after she was born?" She was emboldened. "In ten years, you have never asked to see her." It was fury. For a moment, she also forgot how much the man frightened her—he was the only person in the world she was afraid of.

"I can see my daughter whenever I wish."

"She's at school. She doesn't know you exist."

"She soon will." He looked confident.

"I have work to do."

"I know what your job is. It's to give those men at the *singara* shop a view of your body. I should have always known you were a whore."

"So, it was the cat-voiced *bajiyaa* who told you? Is that what you came to tell me—that I am a whore?"

"No, I came to ask you when the interview is."

"Why should you know of it?"

"I need to prepare for it."

"You aren't a refugee. What makes you think we will take you there?"

"It's simple. I am your husband, and I'll go to America. I want to try having a son one more time with you."

"The third wife didn't do the job either, did she?"

"It must be your curse. It has to be."

"Maybe the problem lies in . . ." She saw the look on his face and cut herself short.

"If I don't get to go to the interview, I shall let the people at the migration office know about your character, your bad character. At least I married you despite your flaws. I should get to go, too. Otherwise, I'll let them know about your ill treatment of my daughters. I have heard these Americans are very serious about violence against children. Violence isn't the answer to everything. Now to discipline a stray woman, maybe."

"You're blackmailing me."

"No, I am not. I married a Bhutanese refugee who gets to go to America. As her husband, I will go, too. Otherwise, they'll know everything. I'll tell them."

"Why would you do that?"

"Simple. I want to be with my family." He broke into a smile. "In America. Maybe I will have a son there—an American son to carry my family name forward."

She looked at her father, and Ravi looked at her. She gave him the date.

At the IOM office, her father needed no prodding.

"Fools—we ethnic Nepali were, big fools," he spat out.

The white woman jotted something. A black reporter from some foreign paper took notes, sometimes asking the white woman to translate what she didn't understand. Just yesterday, documentary filmmakers had tried to interview Anamika. It now seemed like the entire world was suddenly interested in her. Maybe she could tell the woman about her past after all.

"We Nepalese were annoyed that we had to wear the *gho* and *kira*." Her father's teeth were speckled with *khaini*. "Look at me—why should that be a problem? People in India wear Western clothes. Is that a problem? We lived in Bhutan, and *daura suruwal* isn't their national costume. We could have compromised a little."

"So you think the uprising is in many ways the ethnic Nepalese population's fault?" the white woman asked in fluent Nepali.

"Of course, it is." He looked around to spit out his *khaini.* "Look at me—I am a sixth-grade dropout. The Bhutanese government sent me to Japan twice on trainings. I received my promotions on time. My boss at the office still checks on me to see if we need anything."

"Yes, to see if we need anything," Ravi said.

The white woman looked at Anamika. She nodded; her father was speaking the truth about the promotions. She didn't know his boss tried keeping in touch.

Her father continued: "They wanted us to learn Dzongkha. What's the problem with that? If the Drukpas were to settle down in Nepal, they'd have to learn Nepali. We are fools. We like charging at everything with our *khukuri.* Had we thought with our brains, none of this would have happened."

The woman looked at Anamika and then at Ravi, on whose lap sat a clearly uncomfortable Shambhavi. "Suffering, suffering," Ravi said.

Anamika tensed up. Ravi would probably say something stupid. "I don't want to go back to Bhutan," said Anamika. "Not in a hundred years. Not until I die. The country has treated us worse than animals. I am aware of the difficulties resettlement in a foreign country will pose, but I'll learn." Should she share the story of her character? What if they found out later? Would they remove her from the list of refugees selected to move to America?

"That's why we have this interview."

"And I want my daughters to grow up with a country, to know that they won't be removed from another country again."

Ravi interrupted. "Can America ask us to leave, too, like Bhutan did?" He looked at Anamika when he asked the question.

"No, once you've been resettled, which could take more than six months from now, you will get your permanent residency—your green card—in a year. You can apply to be a citizen five years after that."

"Can we leave the country and return as we please?" It was her father.

"Yes, you could, you are as free as any American." She laughed. "Let me warn you, though, that plane tickets are expensive."

"Can we go to Bhutan?" Ravi asked.

Anamika rubbed her big toe on the floor. The man would ruin her.

"If the Bhutanese embassy grants you a visa."

The father looked like he was about to faint. "What has the world come to? We need permission to visit our own country."

"It's better than now," Ravi said. "We don't get to visit it with or without a visa."

This had a calming effect on his father-in-law. "What about our land and property in Bhutan, then?" Ravi asked.

"That we have no control over," the white woman said. "The international community will continue pressuring Bhutan to figure out a solution for repatriation. It ultimately rests on Bhutan."

"Will there be other Bhutanese in our town in America?" Anamika asked. What if a Bhutanese in the town complained to the American police about her character flaws?

"Yes, there will be. If you want to be in the same town as your relatives, we could probably work on that, too."

"No, no, I don't mind being the only Bhutanese in town." That way, her story was probably safe from American authorities.

"No, some voluntary organizations will take care of your needs in the beginning. The organization will also help you out with finding suitable jobs."

Anamika liked the idea of being a useful member of society again. She wouldn't have to depend on anyone for her livelihood after the first couple of months, the white lady had said. Now if only she could get her story out of the way. It had to be done now.

"Is it a problem if one of us in the family doesn't have good moral character?" She was hesitant.

"I don't understand you," the white woman said.

"I am her second husband," Ravi quickly explained. He was about to add something else, but Anamika punched him under the desk. He slapped her hand away. The white woman most definitely noticed.

"We don't care how many husbands you have, Anamika," said the white woman. "What you do in your personal life isn't any of our business."

Ravi got up. Anamika dug the nails of her left hand into her right palm. "What about her?" he asked. "Will she have to wear pants once she moves to America?"

"She can wear anything she wants. It's a free country."

"I'd prefer that she not wear them," he said by way of explanation.

Anamika let out a deep breath when Ravi let matters rest there.

The reporter asked Ravi if she could take a picture of his family. "Only the four of you," she raised her hand with the thumb down, "father, mother, and daughters."

She motioned Diki and Shambhavi to a wooden bench while Ravi and Anamika stood up behind them. "Can you all smile for me?" she asked in a language no one understood.

"*Haasnu rey*," the white woman translated.

The camera whirred and clicked. Once. Twice. Three times.

"Perfect family, perfect picture," the reporter said in Nepali. "Thank you."

THE GURKHA'S DAUGHTER

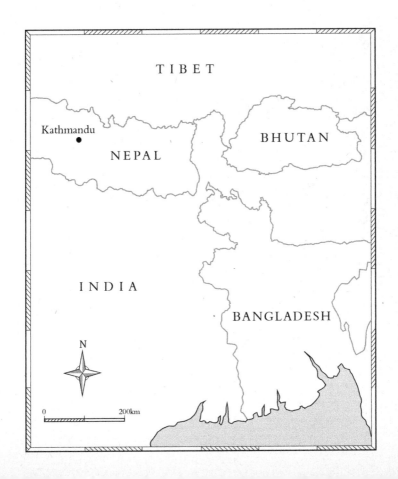

The day after Gita and I combined our miniature kitchen sets, we boasted to the other girls at Rhododendron International Boarding School that we owned a bigger *bhara-kuti* collection than any other nine-year-old in Kathmandu. We had steel utensils, plastic ones, a glass set and gold-plated ones, and these did not include the new set Gurung Bada and Appa had recently sent us from Hong Kong. In addition, Aamaa had, in a charitable mood, given us a few plates—real-life plates—from her kitchen. The glass set we used when we had special pretend guests.

That day, our special guests would be our Gurkha fathers. We'd play our respective fathers and ourselves. Gita had stolen two fake mustachios from Drama Sir's desk in the staff room.

We donned our mustachios, and Gita even wore a black hat. Gurung Bada never wore a hat, but Gita took a little wardrobe liberty. Her Phantom cigarette sweet that dangled between her lips was again out of character—for neither of our fathers smoked—but I didn't mind because she gave me one, too, which I tucked above my ear.

"Give me some beer, Budi." Gita looked back. "And Gita, turn the *jaabo* tape recorder off. Your Appa and Bada are talking."

"Okay, Appa," Gita said in a meek voice, and took off her mustache.

"We are nothing but killing machines to them," Gita spat out, her mustache back on. "They still treat us like dogs."

"No, Numberee, no, don't be angry," I said, not knowing what to add.

"All these years in service, but will they take care of us after that?" Gita said, angry. "No. We will be discarded like socks and shoes. The pension will be worth nothing. How is it that all the other regiments in the British Army get a proper pension? It's only us, brave Gurkhas, who get a fifth of what the others get. Brave indeed! Foolish is what it is."

"Let's count our blessings, Numberee," I countered, stopping my mustache from falling by supporting it with my thumb. "We'd otherwise be in the police, making nothing. What is there to do in this country? We are lucky we got out on time."

"And that McFerron *chutiya*," Gita slurred, taking swigs of water from her miniature glass cup and almost breaking it when she placed it on the ground with force. "He has asked me to bring my drinking down, like it's his father's alcohol I am consuming. Stupid Tommy Atkins that he is—he thinks we are unequal. I haven't created a scene, have I? I haven't picked fights with anyone. I am a peaceful drinker. But the white bastard doesn't think so. I am tired of it."

"Think of it, Numberee," I said, conscious that my part was small and that I wasn't doing a very good job of it. "Our daughters are in a good English-language school. Our wives live well."

"I think I will be the first Gurkha court-martialed because McFerron doesn't like me drinking." Gita was now biting her cigarette sweet. "Bloody English."

"He says he's Irish."

"English, Irish, Scottish—who cares?" She drank some more of the imaginary beer. "They are all the same to me. They all get regular pensions—five times more than we do. It's only we who are inferior to them—we the brave Gurkhas."

"Aamaa, I am hungry," I said, taking my mustache off.

"Yes, Budi, I am hungry, too," Gita said, her mustache still on. "Feed us Gurkhas, feed us brave people and our families, for with the pension we receive, we may be starving a few years from now."

"*Aayo bir Gurkhali*," Gita sang, in an unmistakable imitation of Gurung Bada's voice. It was a song both Gita and I knew— our fathers had taught us. Sometimes, our mothers sang it to us as a lullaby. I joined in as Gita sang one line in her father's voice (with the mustache on) and another in hers (with the mustache off). I tried doing the same, but both my voices sounded similar.

Gita had only the bottom pink portion of her cigarette left.

"Here," I said, breaking mine into half. "You can eat some of mine."

She bit the half into another half.

"Delicious," she said.

"I know," I said, and then back in character again, with the mustache on, I added, "Let's eat all we can here because there is no food like home food. Numberee, this is after so long that both your family and my family are together under the same roof."

"Yes, I know." Gita said, bored now.

I'd need to think of a new character to keep her interested.

"Call the pointy-nosed astrologer," I said. "Call him so we can all see the white hairs covering his ears."

Gita procured two cotton wool balls, spat on them and glued them to her ears. I'd have to try and replay everything the pointy-nosed astrologer had said the day before. A few things, though, Appa and Aamaa warned me, I couldn't even share with Gita, especially with Gita.

The pointy-nosed astrologer had looked at me, back at my birth chart and then let his eyes wander around the rooftop. Exposed iron rods jutted out vertically from the edges of the terrace in desperation, for it would be a long time before we expanded our one-story house into a multistoried one, Appa's dream before he retired from the British Army.

"Here, *naani*, eat this guava and go to play," the astrologer had said to me.

I took the guava, small, green, and hard, and sat still. His order held no real authority, no threat. It was weak, like his voice, and like, as I'd soon discover, my birth chart.

"Not good," he told Appa. "There's a *dosha* on her chart—a kind of *kala sharpa dosha*. She will bring you bad luck for another few years."

Appa frowned, the way he did when I asked him why he took my spot next to Aamaa in bed when he was in Kathmandu. Ever since he came back from Hong Kong on vacation, a slew of astrologers had confirmed what my birth chart clearly stated: that I was unlucky for Appa, that the house would not be completed until I was past fifteen and that I was accident prone and *Manglik*, which meant I'd have trouble finding a man to get married to.

"Bad luck?" Appa said. "What bad luck? I acquired this piece of land after she was born, began building this house after she was born. Those bastard British captains at the regiment began treating me like a human being after she was born."

"All that might be true, but the next few years will be tough." The priest scowled, his forehead wrinkling into six uniform lines. "Let's see—she's nine now. Even after the *dosha* ends, things will continue this way for five or six years. See, I could be like other priests and ask you to do an elaborate *puja*, but I won't."

Aamaa played with the loose end of her purple sari, the one she wore on special occasions at home. When outside, she wore her prettier, shinier silk saris, but inside, she often dressed in this purple one with a purple blouse, the purple-on-purple hiding—or at least taking attention from—the slight tear on her blouse shoulder.

"What is the solution then, Punditjee?" she asked. "I have gone to Manakamana, to Pashupatinath. If you can think of more temples, I will go to them, too."

I bit my guava. It didn't have much of a taste, so I almost threw it away. But I stopped myself because of the religious atmosphere at home. A priest, grains of uncooked rice sprinkled on the birth chart before the priest opened it, and the donning of special clothes convinced me that the fruit, an offering to God first, might be sacred. I balled it into my fist and concentrated on the white hairs sprouting from the pointy-nosed astrologer's ears.

"I don't believe in a *puja* to appease the gods," the astrologer said dismissively. "What we can try to do is shift her bad luck to someone else—preferably a girl her age. Can you think of someone we can bind her in a *miteri* ceremony with? That could change things a little—not a lot, mind you, for there isn't much we can do when one has a *cheena* this bad, and I am not one of those astrologers who believe that the course of a person's fortune can be changed with rituals, but this we can try. I've done it a few times in the past, and it has mostly worked."

Appa, still frowning, asked Aamaa for the red envelope they had earlier readied for the priest, stuffed another fifty-rupee note, bright and crisp, into it and told the pointy-nosed astrologer he'd be in touch shortly.

"I want to settle this problem before I head back to Hong Kong," he said. "I haven't been in any danger since the Gulf War, but they might have some useless war for me to fight again. They are the British after all. And it will be a long time before I am in Kathmandu. Thank you, Punditjee. We cooked quite a feast, but you perhaps don't eat anything cooked by us Magars."

"I am a new-age pundit." The astrologer smiled proudly. "I don't make distinctions based on caste like my fellow priests. As long as you didn't prepare meat, I'll eat everything."

Appa and Aamaa both broke into such wide smiles that I could see Appa's missing molar and Aamaa's gold tooth.

"I'll hurry downstairs and get the plates ready, then," Aamaa said. "We don't cook meat when we invite a priest to the house. Never."

"Yes, and show me the house in the meantime—what little of it is complete anyway," the astrologer asked. "Come, you little one, you unlucky one, let's fill our stomachs before we think up ways to change your life."

I got up, the guava still in my fist, and waited for Appa and the pointy-nosed astrologer to head down the stairs. Using all my strength, I bowled the guava, the same way I saw cricketers on TV do, out on the street, which was at the same level as the terrace, and almost hit a cyclist. He raised his arm menacingly at me. I waved back at him and laughed. The story would definitely make Gita giggle. She'd probably even suggest that we collect all the fallen guavas off the grounds near my half-constructed house and aim them at the steady traffic of pedestrians that went by the terrace. It could be another one of our secrets.

If the pointy-nosed astrologer could predict the future, I wondered if he'd know of my secrets—the smaller one with Aamaa, which Gita and her mother also knew, and the bigger one, the more important one, with Gita. Asking him would just arouse his suspicions. I'd have to ask Gita how to bring it up with him.

Gita was fair and clean and even brushed her teeth at night. She wore a maxi nightdress to bed and could run faster than any of us. She was better at *pittu* than the boys and so often completely toppled the tower of tiny stone slabs with her plastic ball that the boys always wanted her on their team. Gita was Gurung Bada's daughter. Gurung Bada was Appa's close friend from the regiment. Gurung Badi and my mother claimed they were related, but Appa, on more than one occasion, said that wasn't true.

"These Darjeeling women jump to make everyone their relatives—never mind that they are of different castes and have not a drop of common blood," he said a few days ago. "Tomorrow your Aamaa will look for that common blood in me. How can she even consider sharing the same blood as that child devil called Gita?"

I didn't say a word in defense of my best friend's monstrosity and instead conjured up a memory of what she and I had indulged in the day before—Secret Number One, the bigger secret. Would Appa be angry if he found out? Aamaa would be petrified. She had warned me countless times that eating what had touched someone else's mouth would cause boils all over my face. It was even worse than double dipping a samosa. I'd get both my ears pulled. And she'd complain to Gita's mother, who could be a terror. Gurung Badi sometimes even beat Gita with her special stick, a *gauri bet*, the marks of which stubbornly stayed for days. But Aamaa would never find out. Gurung Badi would never find out. It was our big secret, and no one would find out.

It happened the first day of school after the winter break. Gita and I returned to my house from RIBS, our hated school, together. Once we turned eight, because we didn't have to cross a street to get to the institution from my place, our mothers allowed us to walk to and from school by ourselves. Aamaa wasn't in the house, and Appa was never home at this time when he was in the country, so we took the keys from the storekeeper down the street to find a steel bowl of cold Ra-ra waiting for me on the dining table.

"Firstselectiongreen!" Gita shouted once she saw the bowl, grazing the green on the door.

Had she not touched it, I'd have shown her my palm—where I squiggled in green every day for eventualities when the color would be out of reach—and yelled "Firstselectiongreen," winning the opportunity to select between two portions into which I'd now divide the bowl of Ra-ra. Gita might not have employed the trick of wearing the color every day or scribbling with a green sketch pen on her palm, but she still regularly beat me to laying claim on the first selection.

Disappointed at having lost, I pulled a stool to the shelves where the plastic bowls and mugs were stacked. I rinsed a bowl, and carefully, for Aamaa wouldn't tolerate any spills on the dining table, I poured the soup from my bowl to Gita's. Twirling the spoon that Aamaa had left facing downward by the bowl, I cautiously wrapped some curly strands of noodles on it and transferred them to the other bowl while Gita kept vigil to ensure that I wouldn't sneak a spoonful into my mouth. I repeated the process and then stepped back to inspect the two bowls.

The bowl Aamaa had set for me now looked like it hadn't as much of the noodles as the next, so I used my thumb and index finger to pinch some noodles from the plastic container to the steel one. More or less assured that both the bowls now contained equal quantities, I signaled to Gita that I was done with a thumbs-up.

Gita weighed one bowl in her right hand and then the other in her left. She went for the steel bowl, which Aamaa wouldn't have approved of, for no guest, not even ill-mannered Gita, was to eat out of a steel bowl while I used a plastic one, a sacrilege, because plastic was meant strictly for guests.

But that wasn't our big secret.

After we slurped the soup and licked the bowl as deep as our tongues would allow, Gita had an idea.

"Aren't we best friends?" Her pretty blue eyes sparkled.

"Yes, we are."

"Then let's have a little ceremony to prove that."

"What ceremony?" I was excited. It was Gita's idea after all.

"You will spit into my bowl. Spit. Spit. Spit. And I'll spit into yours. Spit. Spit. Spit. And when the bowls are filled to the brim, we shall both drink each other's spit. That way we will have each other in our bodies. We will be real best friends."

Arduous as the task was, we persevered. I generated spit from my throat, from under my tongue and summoned it from the depths of my stomach. Gita, despite having trouble, had already spat out far more than I did. My jaws acted funny, my tongue refused to cooperate, and my mouth felt the way it did when I didn't brush my teeth on nonschool days. I coughed. I choked.

"I think the Ra-ra wants to come out from my stomach," I said, afraid Gita would think me weak.

"Okay, then, this should be enough." Gita gauged the depth of my bowl by inserting her little finger in the sea of spit. "Here, you drink this; I'll drink that."

And with three gulps—she with one, and I with two—we completed our first ceremony to seal our friendship.

If Aamaa found out, she'd probably borrow the *gauri bet* from Gurung Badi to give me the most severe beating of my life.

Would the pointy-nosed astrologer know what we did?

We needn't have undergone the rigorous process of accumulating the last droplet of dribble from our bodies to mark our friendship. Our families, we'd later find out, would have put us through another ritual anyway.

A few days after the pointy-nosed astrologer left with his prediction of doom for me, Appa invited himself and the rest of his family to dinner at Gita's place.

Appa said Gurung Bada was a *jardiyaa*, a drunkard, which wasn't Gurkha-like at all. He often complained to Aamaa about the violent outbursts that accompanied Bada's drinking and about how one of the two white men from the regiment had gotten wind of it and a few times given Bada a talking to.

"The fool is paving the shortest way to his funeral," Appa said to Aamaa as he helped me get into the frilly new dress he had brought from Hong Kong. "Drink a glass or two, but no, we *laureys*, we Gurkhas, think drinking is our birthright. He thinks he can do anything because the Gurkha Sahib likes him. McFerron has threatened to report him to the higher-ups a few times."

Aamaa listened quietly and looked at me, her eyes dancing. We exchanged a smile, a furtive smile between mother and daughter, about Secret Number Two. Aamaa and Gurung Badi often drank together. It was only fair, they'd remark in between gulps of Hit beer, that they be allowed a little release, for their husbands were away, and they were fulfilling the roles of both the parents in the house.

It didn't seem harmful, the way they drank. Gurung Badi and Gita came to our place with a few bottles, and we'd listen to Bollywood songs on our old tape recorder. After a few cups, Gurung Badi danced, which never failed in bringing out peals of laughter from my mother. Gurung Badi was a comical dancer—she tried coordinating Nepali steps with Hindi beats, and no amount of teaching on Gita's part would ever help her mother get it right.

When it was time for them to leave, Gurung Badi would stagger to the door, knocking a flower vase here or a shoe there, and Aamaa always asked her to stay. Gita and I slept together and spent half the night talking about school. Occasionally, we'd hear a giggle from the other room, which made us giggle, too. Drinking didn't seem as destructive as Appa made it out to be.

We weren't about to let Appa know, though—he wouldn't approve. If he frowned on Gurung Bada's drinking, a man's drinking, Aamaa's drinking would probably kill him. It may not have been as big a secret as my saliva exchange with Gita, but I guarded it as I did the bigger secret, promised myself every night—before falling asleep and asking God to take my bad luck away—that no one would know.

Tonight Appa was in the mood to drink.

"We don't get to be together with friends and family this way," he told Gurung Bada. "Your entire family and my entire family are here, Numberee, so tonight I will drink with you."

Appa wasn't even much of a social drinker. All of Aamaa's family made fun of him, even in his presence, for not loving his drink despite being a Magar.

"Our ancestors must have invented the *tongba*," they'd tease. "And here you are betraying your identity and caste."

Appa smiled kindly at them and resumed taking very small sips of his liquor. There'd never be a refill. More often than not, he'd not finish the drink. But tonight he was already on his second glass.

Gita asked Gurung Bada if he had killed anyone on the battlefield. She always asked him that.

Gurung Bada looked at Appa and laughed.

"Killing is bad," he said seriously, and burst out laughing.

"Yes, ask Ghale," Appa said.

"Or Dilley." Gurung Bada guffawed with Appa.

Our mothers looked on indulgently.

"Who are Ghale and Dilley?" Gita asked.

"Yes, Ghale and Dilley," I repeated. "It's like a rhyme."

"Yes, a poem," Gita said.

"Our daughters are such intelligent girls," Gurung Bada said, taking a big gulp and placing the steel glass on the table with a thud.

"Unlike their old men," said Appa. Hoary laughter followed.

"Yes, their old men are brothers. We are brothers."

"You know what, Numberee?" Appa remarked. "We need to seal this relationship with a *miteri*."

"Yes, you and I could be *mit*," Gurung Bada said. "And every one of us will be related."

"No, we are old. We don't need a *miteri* connection. We already have it. How about our daughters? That would be perfect."

Aamaa beamed. Gurung Badi beamed. Gurung Bada looked confused.

"Yes, yes," he said. "Your daughter will be my daughter's *mitini*."

Appa asked for another beer. Gita and I looked shyly at each other. Aamaa let go of the loose end of her shiny new sari—the one with no tear—and hugged Gurung Badi.

I performed my *miteri* ceremony with Gita a week before Appa and Gurung Bada headed back to Hong Kong. Gita and I would be bound in fictive kinship, the bond unifying our families. It was like the gods were listening to our prayers—we sometimes lied to our friends at school that we were cousins.

The pointy-nosed astrologer recommended a simple ceremony, while both our mothers desired to at least invite a couple of neighbors and other Gurkha families. Gita's mother wanted the ceremony at her place, while Aamaa wanted it at ours. When Appa pointed out that we had a terrace conducive to a *havan* and that the blessed pyre of fire was far more convenient to build outside, Gurung Badi complied. Our mothers also wanted to dress us in *guniu-cholo*, but the astrologer thought it was a silly idea.

"They haven't even attained puberty," he said. "That's when you can have a proper *guniu-cholo* ceremony. Dress them in anything you want."

"But in our community, it is different," Gurung Badi declared.

"I am the priest here, so I'd like to do things my way," the astrologer said. "I have to be comfortable. Don't add your own rituals to mine."

Gurung Badi glowered at him. In the end, the astrologer won.

The morning of the ceremony, Gita and I wore our new yellow dresses with butterflies on them that we'd bought with our mothers at the Bishal Bajaar Supermarket. Our dresses were similar except mine had half-sleeves, and Gita chose hers without them. The elders milled around us, hugging occasionally, looking on proudly, each vocally wondering why the good idea of binding us in *miteri* hadn't struck him or her earlier, while the pointy-nosed astrologer read mantras on the opposite side of the sacred fire, into which he intermittently threw rice and *gheeu*. A bright yellow cloth extended from my waist to Gita's. The astrologer from time to time asked us to repeat chants after him and had us cover our heads with our new hankies. We tried suppressing our laughter as the Sanskrit words trickled out of our mouths, halting and unsure.

"It's like being married," I whispered to Gita.

"Yes, but I am the wife because I am wearing a sleeveless dress," Gita explained.

"Yes, you are," I said, accepting.

The astrologer silenced us with a wave of the hand, and we stifled our giggles.

"Gita, please stand up and give the gift you've brought for your *mitini* and do the *dhog* to her." He showed her how to do the *dhog* by bringing his own palms—with his wrinkly fingers pointed upward—together in front of his forehead. "Yes, that's how you do it. You can also do it without smiling. And, you, *naani*, can you please do the same for your *miteri* without laughing?"

We then gave each other five-rupee notes using the astrologer as the medium. I presented Gita a doll that was clothed like her, in a sleeveless dress. Gita looked just like the doll—fair, petite, and beautiful. Gita had brought me a doll, too, big and black. She said her name was Sandy. The astrologer told us that we'd have to summon each other with "Mitini" and not our names from then on. It was all so grand. Wait until the other girls at school heard us call each other Mitini. How envious they would be.

From then on, Gurung Badi would be my Mit Aamaa. I'd have to call Gurung Bada Mit Appa. Gita had to follow the same rules with my parents, which she took to easily. I found it awkward. How could I suddenly change from calling them one thing to another? Calling Gita Mitini, though, was easy. It felt right on the tongue, was the right word for her.

Once we had eaten a vegetarian meal that Gita complained about, she and I rushed outside to collect guavas for some mischief. But first, Gita had to pee.

"I don't like sitting down when I pee," she said conspiratorially. "I'll try peeing standing up. You'll do it with me, too."

I had tried peeing standing up before. It just seemed more convenient than squatting, but the urine just dribbled down my legs and soiled my underwear. I had since stuck to the conventional method.

"Yes, let's do it," I said, sounding excited but afraid of what urinating in this new method would do to my frilly yellow dress. I was a little worried that Gita would get into trouble with Gurung Badi now that my bad luck had been transferred to her.

We went into the bamboo grove, about to be cleared to make way for a house for our new neighbors. As a creature of habit, I squatted.

"No, standing up," Gita ordered.

We lifted our skirts—she her sleeveless one, and I mine with half-sleeves—and pulled down our panties.

"One, two, three, go," Gita said.

Our urine trickled, hesitantly, guardedly. Some of it touched the ground, but most of it soaked our thighs, calves, and feet. Our panties were drenched. Thankfully, we held our new skirts about our waists, so they weren't stained.

"But how do the boys do it?" Gita asked, taking off her underwear and wiping her legs with it. "God promise you won't tell anybody?"

"God promise." I made the sign of a cross near my heart.

She put her underwear back on. Her sleeveless dress looked so good on her.

It was the happiest day of my life. The astrologer was right—my bad luck was probably going away.

I now had three secrets to keep from the world, to think of, and to promise myself never to reveal to anyone before I fell asleep. This was Secret Number Three. No, this was Secret Number Two, while Aamaa's drinking was now Secret Number Three. I'd also need to alter my prayer to God about my bad luck; I'd have to ask him to take Gita's bad luck away.

Peeing standing up wasn't the only act of defiance Gita would commit—she was full of ideas for fresh mischief that would ensure that her luck changed for the worse.

Appa and Gurung Bada left early in the morning two days later. Gurung Badi cried with Aamaa for some time, but Gita and I didn't know the reason, as Aamaa wouldn't allow us in the room. We were already dressed for school because Appa wanted pictures of us in our school uniform.

"Let's go to Swayambunath today," Gita said, pulling me in the direction opposite to the school.

"After school?" I asked her, nervous already, for I knew what the answer would be. My bad luck was her bad luck now, and I'd have to be careful that she was careful. What if Gurung Badi found out?

"No, right now. I don't want to go to that stupid school. I hate Math Sir."

"But how will we get there?"

"We'll ask people. Tell them we live near there."

"But we are in our school uniform. Won't they know that we should be in school?"

"Yes, let's just remove our sweaters." She was wise beyond her years. "We'll look like servants, and no one will guess."

We took off our pullovers, boarded a bus, and changed to another one just when the conductor came near us collecting ticket money. On the next bus, the conductor asked us for money when we got on, and Gita casually paid. I was curious—where'd she get the money?

"God promise you won't tell anyone?" she said.

"Yes, God promise." I made a cross with my finger, mentally numbering this secret. It would depend on how serious it was.

"I took it from Aamaa's purse."

"What if she finds out?"

"She won't. This was just a little of what she had in her purse. She has a lot of money."

"Maybe I'll get some from my Aamaa's purse, too."

"Yes, Mit Aamaa doesn't spend a lot of money. My Aamaa often says that to Appa. She probably has more money than my Aamaa in her purse."

We got off near Swayambunath, where Gita made me circumambulate the stupa and ask God to burn down our school so we'd never have to go again.

Free food was being distributed in one corner, so we stood in line for some *alooko achaar* and *sel-roti*, which we ate off leaf plates.

"Let's go up there and eat," Gita said, pointing to a viewpoint. Swayambunath was located on a hilltop, so we could see all of Kathmandu from various junctures. Gita wanted to use the binoculars, which a suspicious dirty boy, a little older than us, wouldn't allow.

"But we have money," Gita said, waving a hundred-rupee note at him.

"Where are your parents?" the boy asked.

"Inside," Gita said. "Praying."

"I don't believe you."

Gita flashed her tongue at him and called him a monkey.

We ran away, but the boy followed us.

"If I am a monkey," he shouted, "you are a donkey."

He used a word Gita and I weren't allowed to say.

Gita turned around and lunged at him. They both fell down, she on top of him. And then she scratched his face and slapped him a few times.

A group of worshippers gathered around us. A woman tried separating the fighting pair but received a kick from the boy. Hands and legs were everywhere, as were clumps of hair. The pointy-nosed astrologer was right—Gita's luck was worsening. I'd have to ask him what she could do about it. I wouldn't like it, though, if he suggested she get another *mitini* to transfer her ill-luck to.

Finally, a policeman appeared and hit the rolling bodies lightly with his baton.

"How can you behave that way when you are a girl?" he chided Gita.

"How can you hit a girl?" he asked the boy.

"She's a donkey, this girl," the boy said as he got up, his comment prompting a slap from the policeman.

"He tried stealing our money," Gita offered by way of explanation.

"Where are your parents?" the policeman asked.

"We came here in a school group," Gita lied. "Our teacher is waiting for us by the museum. Please don't tell Sir I was fighting. Please. Please. Please. We are late. We need to go."

Before the policeman could say another word, we were running downhill.

"I know," I said when Gita finally looked at me. "God promise." I signed a cross. Two big secrets in a day.

On the *safa tempo* ride back home, we attracted the attention of a middle-aged man.

"Where are you children going?" he asked.

"Memsaab has sent us to get her children from school," Gita cheekily replied. "She also asked us not to talk to strangers."

The man looked at the other passengers and shrugged.

"These people send little girls to pick up little girls," he said to no one in particular. "No wonder we have so many cases of kidnapping."

I expected Aamaa to say something when I got home, thought I'd get a beating, and my ears turned red every time she asked me something about school, but nothing happened. I promised to keep my secrets to myself—five in all, for I lumped the truancy with Gita's fight because the latter happened during the former. I then ranked my secrets in my mind: my spit swapping with Gita was still the most treasured secret, second was the Swayambunath episode with Gita, third was Gita's theft, which was followed by peeing standing up with Gita, and Aamaa's drinking was relegated to Secret Number Five. The secret about the *mitini*—the one the pointy-nosed astrologer asked me to be quiet about—wasn't really a secret because it didn't involve Gita.

No one questioned our absence in school the next day, but Gita then returned to school with unmistakable *gauri bet* marks. Gurung Badi had found out her daughter was a thief. Maybe my bad luck was rubbing off on my *mitini* after all.

I turned ten on April 30, 1997, ten days before Gita did. Aamaa said that I couldn't have a birthday party because of the unpredictability in Appa's life right now. Appa and Gurung Bada might soon have to move to another country from Hong Kong, she said. No one was sure if they'd be transferred to Brunei or the UK, but Aamaa went to Pashupatinath a lot these days.

The pointy-nosed astrologer made more trips to our place than he had in the past. He often asked me if my luck had changed, to which I didn't know the answer. Gita did get more beatings from her mother than before, so my luck must have changed. I asked the astrologer what she could do to change her luck, to which he remarked there was nothing she could do and that I'd have to keep the actual reason for our ceremony a secret from her. I wasn't about to make it Secret Number Whatever—my rankings were in a mess because Secret Number Three, Gita's stealing from her mother, was no longer a secret.

Something important was about to happen, and if the astrologer's increased visits didn't prove it, Aamaa and Gurung Badi's hushed talks, during which Gita and I were banished outdoors, definitely did. They talked about this impending transfer as much as they predicted the content of Gurung Badi's bulging tummy. Inquisitive, I went to the one person who had an answer for everything.

"Don't you know?" Gita asked. "China is taking back Hong Kong."

"Really?" I said, faking comprehension.

"Yes, and because your Appa and my Appa both work for the British, they will have to go, too."

"Go where?" I asked. It was even more complex. I wondered how Gita made sense of everything.

"To Britain. The UK and Britain are the same country, Mitini. Or to Brunei—my Appa is going to London, but your father has been transferred to Brunei."

"Yes, I know that," I lied. "I wasn't sure that Appa would go to Brunei."

"Of course they will, and Aamaa says we are going, too. She says we can live much better in the UK than in Hong Kong. She has also had enough of taking care of two children—one me, and my little sister in her stomach—and needs a husband's help now."

It made sense. Just the day before, I heard Gurung Badi tell Aamaa that she wanted to kill Gurung Bada.

"They do their thing and are gone—fools," she said. "They don't know what we go through for nine months and then after. We are worse off than widows. I don't even want another child."

"But we are here." Aamaa was sympathetic. "We can take care of you to some extent."

"Yes, but an absent husband is as good as having no husband. Once the baby is born, I will ask him to take us all away. I don't care how we live there, but I am going. I will otherwise let him know that I will never allow my son to join the service."

"How do you know it's a son?" I asked, momentarily forgetting Aamaa's rules of decorum that entailed never interrupting when elders talked about something serious. And this, I knew, was serious.

"Oh, I know it is—only a son could give me so much trouble. All he does is kick and kick and kick. He's already giving me more problems than his father."

Before Aamaa could say something, I volunteered to excuse myself.

I prayed to God, for Gita's sake, it would be a daughter, a young sister she could dress up. I wondered if the pointy-nosed astrologer would know the sex of the baby.

"I think she will be as pretty as you," I said to Gita.

"Yes, and she'll only wear sleeveless clothes," Gita declared. "In the UK, the clothes will be so much cuter."

I prayed we'd join Appa, too—if not in the UK, at least in Brunei.

"In the UK, there is no mud," Gita said. "Everything is so clean, and I can wear so many sleeveless dresses."

Gita had cousins who lived in the UK, and they occasionally sent her pictures. She carefully studied these photos and developed her own sartorial sense based on them. She cut out a heart on her shirt to show off the mole above her chest and had even asked her mother for a nose piercing, but Gurung Badi wouldn't have any of that.

"I will get a piercing once I am in the UK," Gita promised. "All Gurung girls have it. Aamaa wants me to grow a little before I can get it, but I want it now. I am almost ten. I am old enough."

I undressed Sandy, the big, black doll Gita had given me, and dressed her again. I undressed her and dressed her again. Dress. Undress. It didn't seem like the astrologer had succeeded in ridding me of my bad luck.

"We will take a plane and land on top of Mount Everest for tea," Gita said, animated. "Aamaa even says I can drink some beer."

I wondered if Gita picked Sandy for me because I looked like her, just as I had picked the fair, beautiful doll for her because she looked like Gita.

"No rice anymore, thank God," she said. "Only bread and butter and cakes. And I will eat with chopsticks. Renu didi told me that's what they use there."

"What are chopsticks?" I asked.

"Sticks to eat everything with. That's what they use in Hong Kong, so that's what they eat with in London, too. Maybe I will send you some as a gift."

"Yes, and I can eat with them here, but who will teach me?" I asked hopefully.

"Ask your Appa to when he comes home on vacations. And I will get a new *mitini*. You should get a new one, too, now that we won't live in the same place."

It was all I needed to run crying to Aamaa. I was losing my best friend, and *she* was the one—the one who now had my bad luck—going to a magic land.

Aamaa said we were staying simply because I'd receive a better education than I'd get in Brunei, where Appa would be transferred.

"They treat us badly there," she said, like she'd been there. "All Gurkha children go to the camp school. Here, you go to an English-language school."

"How can that be?" I asked. "But Gita is going to the UK."

"In the UK, they can study in English schools, but in Brunei you can't."

"Then why can't Appa go to the UK?"

"Because he wasn't transferred there. Don't worry—Gita will suffer. She won't be able to understand the way they speak in English in the UK."

So, Gita was unlucky. Then why did I feel miserable? The pointy-nosed astrologer would definitely ask me not to think about such things and concentrate on my math instead.

Things are blurry after that. I think Appa came home a few months after Gita left, or it could have been weeks. He had grayed around the temples and looked smaller than I remembered him. He had completed fifteen years in the army and had hoped for a few years of extension or permission to work in the UK, but neither happened. Gurung Bada, according to Appa, wouldn't retire anytime soon because he had made himself the Gurkha Sahib's absolute favorite. All of McFerron's complaints went unheeded because the Gurkha Sahib himself liked alcohol as much as Gurung Bada did.

Thankfully, I had something else besides Sandy the doll to remember Gita by. She had left all her *bhara-kuti* behind. Gurung Badi wouldn't allow her to take the little utensils because they would eat up space in their luggage. I barricaded myself from the newfound tension brewing between Appa and Aamaa by selecting various combinations of plates, pots, and pans and using them in my solitary games on the terrace.

"I am retired," I said in Appa's voice. I put my mustache on and drank from a small steel cup, chipped at the edge. "I get a pension."

"A pension of not even ten thousand rupees." I removed the mustache. "We can barely pay for her school with that. You can try something—be a bodyguard or a security."

Mustache on.

"I am a retired Gurkha. I belong to a regiment that has won thirty-six Victoria Crosses. Do you think I can go around looking for jobs as a security guard?"

Mustache off.

"Then how will we make ends meet? Forget your dream of adding floors to the house. Forget everything. You're not even thirty-five. We have a life ahead of us."

Mustache on.

"Don't worry. We will be granted British citizenship. We can then all go to the UK and work."

Mustache off.

"How long will we wait? By then all our savings will be gone. Is this what you get for all these years of service, of living away from your family?"

Mustache on.

"I am with my family now."

I forgot to take the mustache off.

"Then I was happier when you were not here. At least we weren't worried about what we would eat. I am tired of living in this half-completed house."

Mustache still on. Phantom cigarette between the lips.

"It will happen soon. The British are kind people. They wouldn't turn us away. We have fought with them for more than two hundred years. It will happen soon. And soon, we will all live there."

Appa waited for a long time, his faith unwavering. He had little to do with his days. He'd go to meetings with other Gurkhas. There were so many of them—the Gurkhas and the meetings. Sometimes, they convened at our place. Hope and frustration mingled with song, dance, and alcohol, which Appa these days consumed more and more.

Several months of idleness later, Appa one day came home with the news that he had been offered a job as a personal security guard to a businessman, some Golcha man.

Aamaa smiled for the first time in a long while. To celebrate, we had chicken and mutton for dinner, and although I thought I'd want to stay with them, I found myself, more so when I observed Appa, hankering to retreat to my *bhara-kuti*.

Today, there'd be some improvisation. Instead of Phantom cigarette sweets and a mustache, I'd use one of the two smaller knives from Appa's *khukuri* set. He had given me the knives only two days ago to decorate my room. He told me to be careful with them, not to use them for anything but decoration. I was ecstatic because Appa didn't allow anyone—not even Aamaa—to come near his *khukuri* set, even when it was sheathed. He always said that it was a part of his uniform and that nothing gave him more pride than cleaning it himself. When asked why he was giving me his favorite toy, his Sandy, he said he had no use for it.

"I'll take it," I said in Appa's voice, and sliced the air with one of the knives. "He's paying me twenty thousand rupees. I will be his personal security guard."

"That's great news." I smiled from ear to ear. "We can finally add the floor upstairs. And it's prestigious."

"Yes, very prestigious." I stabbed the air with a knife. "He says it's a good thing I know how to drive."

"Maybe he has plans of buying you a car." I smiled from ear to ear.

"I think he might have me drive him around." I steered an imaginary wheel with the knife.

My eyes popped out, the way I had seen Aamaa's when I lied to her.

"A Gurkha driving?" I said. "I don't believe it. Well, we can always keep the driving part away from the people."

"Yes, they won't know." I dug the knife in the mud. I tried cracking my knuckles. I couldn't.

I didn't like this knife prop. I'd have to change my game.

The red telephone, which was from Gita's set, rang.

"Tring, tring," I sang.

"Hello, Mitini, but you didn't send me a letter." My voice was back. "Never mind, never mind. Don't say sorry. You're my *mitini*—you shouldn't be saying sorry. Appa and Aamaa are smiling now, but I don't think Appa is very happy."

I talked for some time and felt considerably better.

After Gita, there were Sunita and Monica at school—nice girls who wouldn't think of playing truant or fighting a street urchin—and after them there was a boy, whom I don't want to remember. He caused me a lot of pain, even called me names. Gita would never do that.

Sunita and Monica came to see my *bhara-kuti* collection one day after school. They were impressed at the size of the cylinder and the beauty of the glass set. I gave Sunita the red phone and Monica a gold-plated cup. When they left, I took a big plastic bowl left to dry by the sink and spat into it with all the effort I could muster. That day, I spat a little more than I had the day before.

I placed the bowl on Sandy's big, black mouth, counted to ten, asked her why she couldn't finish the drink in one gulp and emptied the bowl into the bushes.

I'd have to ask the pointy-nosed astrologer when he came next if sealing friendships in a different way—in ceremonies that were not the *miteri*—successfully transferred a girl's bad luck to her best friend. He would have something silly to say, but I didn't need to bother. Like Appa dismantling his *khukuri* set, I, too, had no need for Sandy anymore. Maybe I'd give her to Sunita. Or Monica. It didn't matter to whom. Or I could simply rip the doll's arms and legs apart and bury her in the ground. I could always use Appa's tiny knife, now useless to him, to dig the grave.

Passing Fancy

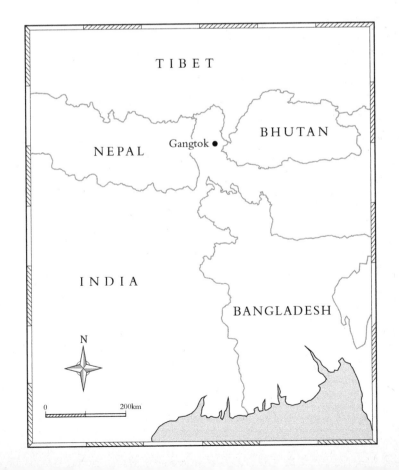

Her son Rakesh ended up going to America after all. The night they saw him off at the Indira Gandhi International Airport, both she and her husband cried. They hadn't done it before; they didn't even go all the way to Delhi to say good-bye to Sachin, their firstborn. Sachin maintained that having them accompany him would trigger a flurry of tears, and he wasn't prepared to let emotional upheavals get in the way of the start of an event as major as a new life in America. Latha had simply shaken their hands as she prepared to part ways. When her mother tried drawing her into an embrace, Latha moved back, and for a second they stared at each other, the hands unsure about their role in the hug. The wife had waited for her husband to either cry or say something deep when the sight of a bawling garland-clad young man, probably a student like Latha, surrounded by a bevy of sniveling middle-aged ladies drew their attention. Father, mother, and daughter stood around laughing, all secretly thankful that the farewell in their family was a relatively unemotional affair. It was a tension-free moment.

With Rakesh, however, the tears flowed uncontrollably. It had been an agonizing couple of hours. Rakesh was leaving by a midnight flight, and the conversation at the eight p.m. dinner, extremely late by their standards, was already quiet and stilted.

They talked about the insipid daal, the harangued waiter, and the rudeness of Delhi people. No one mentioned America. No one mentioned Rakesh's leaving. When Rakesh finished dessert and asked if he could possibly have one of the gold rings his mother was wearing, to sell it should a situation sufficiently dire arise, she broke down first. The husband asked her to control herself, to be aware that their son wasn't going to war. He told Rakesh he was more than welcome to return if he didn't like it in America. He needn't think about the money spent, the year wasted, and what people would think back home. And he shouldn't ever worry about money. Yes, without doubt one of the reasons they were sending him abroad was for him to become financially responsible, but if he had difficulty finding a job to pay for school from the second year onward, he must let them know.

Rakesh told his parents to have faith in him and that he wouldn't ask them for more money no matter what. They had, after all, paid for an entire year's education in his case, as opposed to only a semester for his brother and sister. He was nervous, but wasn't everyone, even cocky Latha? He knew they thought he was slow, stupid even. And yes, he didn't have the best examination scores. He always was the slowest among all his friends to grasp concepts, but that didn't mean he was an idiot. He took a long time with his lessons but also took a long time to forget them. He still remembered all his fourth-grade poems he had spent hours memorizing—"Down in a green and shady bed, a modest violet grew"—along with a truckload of useless information he had always had trouble understanding.

This was a long speech, coming from someone like Rakesh. It was devoid of self-pity, and nothing he said insinuated that their parenting skills were lacking, but the wife, translating his words into their failing of him, sniffled. The son had known all along their doubts about him. He might have been the slowest of their three children, but he was the most perceptive. He talked about one of his dreams of wanting to surprise them by doing well, maybe even better than Latha. When this only elicited a snuffle from his mother, he said he did not want them to think they had been bad parents. They had been excellent. He confessed he had been ambivalent about reassuring them that he would be okay, aware that when words came tumbling out of his mouth, he got excited, even aggressive, and often gave the wrong impression, and he had just succeeded in doing exactly that. He was sorry, he said several times, and every time he apologized, memories of the past came pounding in the wife's conscience—of multiplication tables gone horribly wrong for the fourteenth time, of never-ending family jokes generated out of something he said, and the exaggerated laughter when they hunted for the humor in his anecdotes. The tears lasted all the way to the airport, where Rakesh, trying again to inject some last-minute humor into a hopeless situation, said he was confused about whether or not to cry. It was said with absolutely no malice, and the sincerity with which he was trying to raise their spirits, when it should have been vice versa, was heartwarming, so both decided—the wife pressed by a pinch from the husband when she tried swallowing a sob—that they should stop until he left, two seconds after which the wife's eyes set to work again. They had never been that way.

"That's the third one gone," said the wife when sobs gave way to words.

"You thought he wouldn't go."

"I hoped he wouldn't go." She watched the sky for Rakesh's plane.

"I am mighty proud he went. He'll learn. He'll see the world. It will do him good."

"Some people survive and live without being battered and bruised by the universe." Her tone was hostile.

"You talk like I had something to do with encouraging him to go. I just thought his life would be a lot better if he went abroad."

"He once told me he'd be happy if he went to college in India."

"He could have, but he chose not to."

"You never know about the bettering of life. For all we know, he might be moneyed and miserable."

"You wish I had stopped him from going, don't you?"

"You're always so manipulative." She still saw no plane in the sky. "I thought you'd give it at least one shot. I know you've had as much doubt about whether he can survive the harsh world out there."

"Didn't I say that would be a selfish thing to do? We'd be limiting his options. Let him first go see what's out there and make up his mind. He can always come back."

"I can imagine his brother quitting his studies and coming back if he doesn't like it. I can see his sister returning midway if she feels like it. But we both know this one will not come back even if he hates his life. He'd feel too guilty. He's too simple."

"Simple, slow, silly—that's all you think he is, we think he is." The husband's exasperation showed. "That's one of the reasons he's this way. He has been protected all his life, and we are to blame. Our notion that he's too simple, too foolish, to experience anything, to fend for himself, to go out there and see what he wants out of life has already caused him enough trouble. At least let him be for some time now. Let him make his own mistakes and learn from them. The way you talk about him, you'd think he's an autistic child. Stop it. He's a nice, normal human being. He keeps getting compared to his brother and sister. That's it. He's less academically inclined than they are and not a retard."

"Don't get angry. You're right, I worry needlessly about him."

"Then let's drop the topic."

"Okay," the wife said quietly as a plane—was it Rakesh's?—ascended.

"I sometimes really wonder if you are actually afraid for him or for yourself. I understand that you feel more and more purposeless as each child leaves. I feel the same way. It feels like our children don't need us anymore, but I don't try to stop them from going after what they want."

They stared at the sky until the plane diminished into a little ball of fire and vanished altogether.

A month after Rakesh left, the wife retired from her government job. She had hoped to extend the length of her service by another year, but her political leanings favoring the opposition party complicated matters. She had on many occasions told her family, her brothers, and cousins that she'd sleep until noon the first Monday after retirement. She'd then play cards with her husband—and any of her children still around—before eating breakfast or completing her ablutions. She joked that if she were a man, she'd grow stubble, never wear a tie again, except maybe at one of her children's weddings, and devour all the books that she had for so long had no time to read. She would hole herself up in her husband's cavernous library to revisit the Leo Tolstoys that she had purchased as a twenty-two-year-old and brought with her to this house when she got married but of which she hadn't gone beyond the first few pages. She wasn't going to travel for at least six months. As it was, her husband wasn't very fond of traveling—he said sitting in a cramped space with his knees going clang-bang-bang against the back of someone else's seat, even if the trip meant seeing all his children, made him claustrophobic. The wife had expressed interest in visiting America several times, and he had told her he wouldn't mind her going alone. She had stopped bringing up the subject these days.

The first Monday after retirement panned out differently. She woke up at five a.m. and went for a walk, her first in more than twenty-five years. Right next to the Titanic Park, before she took the overpass, she saw Mr. Bhattarai, her neighbor, greeted him, and stopped to talk. What did she plan to do after the walk, for wasn't it her first day of living like a queen, after all? Mr. Bhattarai teased. Oh, she'd probably go back home and watch TV. It wasn't like she had anything to do all day anyway. Mr. Bhattarai asked her about her travel plans as he unzipped his jacket and fanned himself. She described in great detail the time her husband, a nervous flyer, embarrassed her by repeatedly chanting the Gayatri Mantra, much to every passenger's chagrin, when they flew from Delhi to Bagdogra. She was in no great hurry. She didn't have a job to dress up for or Rakesh's early-morning slowness—exacerbated by the two-week-old sports section of the *Statesman* glued to his eyes while his roti got cold—to run home to. She wondered aloud if Mr. Bhattarai knew that Rakesh had left, too. Yes, he did know that, wasn't it England or Australia? No, America, like the rest. Didn't he find it strange no one wanted to study in India? Almost every household had at least one child abroad. That was stretching it, he replied with a smile. What was strange was the number of doctors in every household, thanks to the new medical college in town. Anyone could become a doctor, just about anyone, he said. She had to agree. Yes, he was right, going abroad for studies was yet to grip Sikkim the way it had the rest of India, but doctors . . . yes, students who could barely pass their high school exams found themselves in medical schools. A pity, he added, because he didn't trust his wife's young doctors. She wasn't comfortable talking about his sick wife, so she made some excuse about her husband's breakfast and walked home.

She felt restless. She had nothing to do. The servant didn't take very kindly to her being in the kitchen when she went to see if he needed help. His territory, she considered. She played solitaire on the computer for some time—just three months ago, she had finished her basic computer classes—and checked her e-mail. Her children hadn't replied to any of her mails. That was typical. Did it cost them money to send replies? You never knew— after all, America was expensive. Or maybe they were just busy. Still, a one-line reply wouldn't hurt. Latha sometimes replied "ha-ha" to her mother's carefully constructed messages detailing the dogs' antics and her husband's cheating shenanigans at cards. If a big scoop found its way into her e-mails, like the time a relative's servant was found pregnant, Sachin would call immediately. It was Rakesh—gone for only a month—out of whom extracting a response was the most difficult. He never checked his Hotmail, he said. The one time he called, he had very little to say, worrying her endlessly about whether he was happy.

"Nothing from anyone?" her husband asked, standing behind her, the dogs at his heels.

"What do you expect?"

"Not even Latha?"

"No."

"They must be busy."

"All we want to know is that they're fine."

"If they aren't fine, they probably will call us."

"The others have been gone years. It's Rakesh I am worried about."

"Didn't we just talk to him a week ago?"

"But he was quiet. We did all the talking."

"As we should."

"Yes, I am worrying needlessly."

"You have more time to think now than you did before."

"I should probably start reading again."

"Let's play a round first," the husband said, shuffling the pack of cards.

*   *   *

When the wife saw Mr. Bhattarai again during her morning walk, he waved at her. She had the dogs with her today, and they were pulling her in opposite directions. Two huge Alsatians stubbornly involved in a tug-of-war as she tried to control them must have made for a silly sight. Mr. Bhattarai ran to her and ordered the dogs in a loud, booming voice to sit down, and they strangely did as they were told. He asked her about her retirement. She knew she should keep quiet, but she confided it was depressing. There was nothing to do all day, and the robot—that's what they called a servant in the family, ha-ha—was impatient when she entered the kitchen. She had initially thought she'd read a lot but realized now how out of touch she was. She'd read page after page, and the words felt welcoming but barely registered. What books was she reading? Oh, Tolstoy. He suggested she start with a lighter book. She was always a reader when young, she replied. Then *restart* with something light, he reworded himself, a book whose lines she didn't have to go through over and over again. She asked for suggestions. He couldn't think off the top of his head, but there had to be something. How about Mills & Boons? She laughed at his idea and asked about his familiarity with romance novels. Oh, no, no, he began reading them when Manju was in the hospital—light and fluffy stuff, just the books that didn't require too much energy for him to become engrossed in. Once she was habituated, rehabituated, she could graduate to heavier material.

She wondered if she should bring up the topic of his wife. This must be one of those few times he must not think of the sick woman, so she decided against mentioning her. He asked her what her husband did all day. Oh, they spent most of the day playing cards. They sometimes gambled for minuscule amounts of money—of course, his money was her money, so there wasn't really anything at stake, but they were both sore losers and were in it to win—and often played for household chores. Although their robot, who had been with them for a decade and a half, could take care of all the cleaning and cooking, they liked to set aside a list of chores for themselves to do. It helped pass time and made them feel they weren't whiling their lives away. With the children in America and her retirement, she felt useless.

He opened his mouth to say something but stopped before he started the sentence. She sensed it was about his wife. Had she tried helping the neighborhood children with their home-work? he asked. It helped pass time. It was what he did when he first retired. That would take care of time after the children's school hours. He'd think up a list of things for her to do. How about, for example, learning how to use the computer and writ-ing e-mails to her children? Oh, she already did that and was tired of logging in and logging out three, sometimes four, times a day. The children seldom sent prompt replies, and there she was, trying to make her e-mails as relatable and interesting to them by including everything from the robot's temper tantrums to the dogs' mischiefs. It was impressive a woman her age knew how to use a computer; it had taken him, a retired engineer, many, many weeks to learn it, after years of pestering from his sons abroad. Oh, yes, even his sons were in America. They were a big inspiration to her children. Yes, with the children gone now, he had been painting these days when his wife took long five- to seven-hour naps during the day. That must be nice, she said. Yes, yes, it was nice—he wasn't very good, but he wouldn't mind showing her his paintings. How about she stop by one of these days? She'd love to.

Her husband saw her reading a Mills & Boon novel and asked with a chuckle what she was doing reading trash.

"Soon you'll want the kind of man described in those books," he said. "I'll be inadequate."

"How do you know how they're described?"

"You know, tall, dark, and handsome. Maybe I should've been darker."

"You've probably read them yourself. How do you know how the men are described in there?"

"Naah, I don't read trash. It poisons your mind. Whatever happened to your big plans of studying Tolstoy?"

"I haven't read in so long; I think I should start with something lighter."

"Yes, like *Tinkle* comics." He was in a jovial mood. "Or Pinki. Or Chacha Chaudhary. Remember how much Rakesh loved them?"

"Yes, I also remember how many times he missed the school bus because he'd not stop reading them."

"He called today. I asked him if he found Chacha Chaudhary comics in America."

"Why didn't you tell me he called?"

"We don't see each other very often, which is funny because we both have nothing to do," he said.

Her husband was right. He wasn't yet awake when she went on her walks. He liked to run in the evenings and tried to get her to do the same, but she found herself up at five every morning and didn't know what to do; going on a walk was the best way to kill time. And she had been so engrossed in her romance novels the last couple of days that they hadn't played cards at all.

She had missed her son's call while she was busy making conversation with a man who wasn't her husband. The memory of Mr. Bhattarai trying to make the two Alsatians sit made her smile.

"What'd he say?" she asked.

"The usual."

"Does he need money?"

"He didn't mention it. I did most of the talking."

"Should I just put some money into his account? You know, as a security blanket?"

"Why would you do that?" He was irate. "He hasn't asked for it."

"Just so—"

"No," he said firmly. "We'll not give him any money. If he needs something, he should learn to ask."

"That he never will."

"Let him learn then."

"So, you want him to starve in a foreign land?"

"Yes, let him do that. If that will teach him to be a man, so be it. Your love is the reason he's this way."

She would deposit two hundred thousand rupees into Rakesh's account that her husband, who had already procured a pack of cards from the drawer, didn't need to know about. Rakesh was the youngest, after all. She found herself wondering what method other parents employed to help out their children abroad. She was going to find out tomorrow.

Mr. Bhattarai asked her where the dogs were. Oh, they created too much trouble and hampered her speed walking. Maybe they need someone like him to discipline them, she said, turning scarlet. Yes, his father was an army man, and he was brought up with an iron hand. One grain of rice on the table, and he'd have his ears boxed. He laughed. She laughed. But he didn't have the heart to be too strict with his boys. Yes, neither she nor her husband was very good with disciplining—they tried but always failed. If she had had her way, she wouldn't have sent any of her other children abroad after the eldest dissipated her glamorous notion associated with foreign studies through his descriptions of trysts with illegal jobs. Children abroad—nothing parents said ever dissuaded them from chasing the dollar dream, right?

she said. Yes, she was similar to him because even his children were abroad, and he understood her concerns.

Did his children ever ask for financial support? She wanted to help her youngest out even if he hadn't asked for any money, but her husband was opposed to it. Yes, the older one asked for help in his family, and they had to provide him with it. The younger one was responsible. He was even ready to pay back the money they had given him in the beginning. Oh, it was just the opposite with her children. She wasn't particularly worried about the older ones—they were responsible and ambitious. The youngest, though, didn't talk so much. Sure, he hadn't been gone for long, but she was always anxious for him. What if he began drinking and smoking? She knew she had to let go, but it was impossible, no matter how hard she tried. Did the thoughts of his children keep him awake at night?

No, he said. Losing sleep over her grown-up son would get her nowhere, and as far as drinking went, she should wake up and see the world around her—every teenager was doing it, so it wouldn't be criminal for her son to indulge in it once in a while; it wasn't unhealthy. See, she came from a family of unhealthy people. How did he manage to stay so fit? He had the health of a twenty-year-old. He smiled and said it was the early-morning walks and good conversationalists that kept him young. She turned red at his using "conversationalists" instead of "conversations." He understood she was afraid of alcoholism and addiction, but if her son was drinking in moderation—and he probably was—it wasn't any cause for worry. No, it would concern her and her husband, she remarked. No one in their family drank, not even a sip of wine, and they had brought up their children with the right values, but there were temptations everywhere, especially abroad, although, yes, she hadn't been outside India. But one man's meat is another's man's poison, he said. Didn't values differ? She didn't quite understand. He'd try to give examples—yes, he had a great example, but she shouldn't be offended. He drank, yes, and so did his sons, and yes, they'd drink together if they visited. Together? She was surprised. Yes, didn't she think that was unacceptable? He wasn't surprised. But he and his sons would be equally horrified if they saw her and her husband playing cards, gambling with their children. Now, that would be taboo in their house. Okay, another example. In some families, married women mingle freely with other men while in other families, that would cause a lot of alarm. What kind of family was his? she asked, even though she knew what the answer was. It didn't matter, he said, because no one knew who he was talking to in the mornings. No, no, no, she said, she didn't mean it that way. He knew what she meant, and yes, her husband was right—sending the money to her son would only make him more dependent on them.

Her husband was ready with a pack of cards when she got home.

"Higher to deal," he said, picking up a card from the deck. He had a nine. "Let's play Kitty."

She picked her card: a king. She dealt.

"Are we playing for chores?" she asked.

"There's nothing to do. Let's play for money."

"How much?"

"A hundred rupees—same rules."

"That's a lot of money, don't you think? It's real gambling."

"Since when did the high stakes begin bothering you? All of us are big gamblers, even Rakesh."

"I wonder what people say about that."

Her first two hands were excellent—a straight flush and a straight. Her last hand was weak, but she needed just two hands to win the money.

"About gambling? Everyone knows that we are a family of gamblers."

"I wonder if people judge us for it."

"We don't judge others who play cards, do we?"

"But we judge people who drink." She did not want to bring it up, but she couldn't help herself.

"Drinking isn't the same as cards," he said defensively.

"To some people it's worse. Drinking is a part of so many cultures. It's not a vice to people belonging to these cultures, but gambling could be."

"Do you not want to play cards?" the husband asked, defeated.

"I do."

"Then let's stop talking about what's bad and what's not. Ready?"

"Yes, I dealt, so you show first." He showed three jacks—that beat her straight flush. She'd probably lose.

"Aha, I have a feeling I will win," the husband, excited, shouted. He clenched his fists and threw his arms in the air.

Mr. Bhattarai's older son had applied for a green card and was waiting for its approval. Oh, then wouldn't he, as the father, also get a visa easily? He might, but what use was it to him? He had to look after his wife, whose condition wouldn't be the same it was two years ago no matter how hard the doctors worked. How was his wife? Well, she had stopped growing violent the last week or so, but she still didn't recognize him, or anyone, for that matter. How did he manage to stay so cheerful despite fate dealing one blow on him after another? He couldn't change some things; what he could do was change his attitude toward them. No, no, to have a wife—she hunted for the words—whose condition was rapidly deteriorating, with little hope for improvement, must be difficult. Didn't he ever want to break away from it all?

It was a dangerous question, too personal, with too many implications for two people who were not each other's spouse.

Mr. Bhattarai seemed unperturbed. Yes, of course, it was difficult, and not a day went by without his thinking of breaking away. His children tried persuading him to admit his wife into a nursing home, where she'd receive round-the-clock care, and he would be lying if he said he wasn't tempted every so often to commit her to one of these new homes mushrooming in Siliguri, but he was afraid of what society would say. And, yes, she should come to his place anytime to see the paintings. He had painted all day yesterday. It was a nice painting that she'd definitely love, he added, continuing to look her in the eye. She noticed his eyeballs were really light.

"Mrs. Bhattarai seems to be doing better," she said, grimacing at her terrible cards.

"You mean she's not trying to murder people?" the husband asked.

"Apparently her violent outbursts have stopped."

"That's good. Any other improvements?"

"Her husband says she still doesn't recognize him."

"That fellow is a strong man. He's been taking care of her for three years."

"And he never complains," she added.

"How would we know that?" he said. "We aren't best friends. He probably complains about his sorry life with someone he's close to."

She wondered what her husband would say if she told him about her early-morning talk with Mr. Bhattarai. She was certain he would be horrified were he to hear Mr. Bhattarai talking about sometimes thinking a nursing home was acceptable for his wife. She was suddenly conscious that she wanted Mr. Bhattarai to look good to her husband. It was odd—what should she care what her husband, or anyone in the world, thought of this man?

"His sons think they should admit her into a nursing home."

"Who in these parts of the world does that?" her husband asked crossly. Clearly, he didn't have very good cards.

"She's better now, but when she was violent, don't you think she'd have been better off at the nursing home?"

"Nursing homes in India are moneymaking rackets," he said. "I don't think a nurse would take very good care of her."

"At least they wouldn't have to worry about her hurting people then."

"Would you like it if our children admitted us into old-age homes when we're old?" the husband said.

"I would. In fact, I am thinking of talking to them about it."

"And what would your explanation to the world be?"

"Simple. That I don't want to be a burden on my children."

"And be a laughingstock? Anyway, do you think the children would admit us?"

"I think they will."

She won the first of three hands; her cards weren't as bad as she thought.

"No, only Sachin would. He's pragmatic and selfish. Latha would not. Rakesh most definitely would not."

"If Mr. Bhattarai's sons think it's all right for their mother to be admitted into a nursing home, why shouldn't our children?"

She won the second hand, too.

"Because we brought them up the right way."

"Why are you vilifying the poor man?" she asked.

"No, I am not saying he's evil. I think his sons are evil."

"But maybe the sons want to relieve the father of his burden."

"And after the father gets rid of their mother, what? Will they ask him to get another wife? Or worse, will they do the same to him when he's sick?"

"I want you to admit me into a nursing home if we come to a situation in which I can't make a decision for myself."

She didn't care who won the third hand; she had already won the round and wasn't concerned about the bonus that winning all three hands would bring. But she loved beating her husband, so when she saw her third hand was better than his, she pumped her fist in victory and picked up the two hundred-rupee notes lying by the deck.

"I seriously thought I'd win at least two hands," he said.

"Give me my *salaami*, too."

"How about I admit you now?" he said, unsurely handing her another hundred-rupee note. "You're talking like a person who needs to be admitted in an asylum. You deal."

She went to see Mr. Bhattarai's art one particularly boring Saturday. She'd have called, but she didn't have his number. In an attempt to look a little different, she had tied her hair in a tight bun, saw that it attracted attention to the vermilion in her parting, and then let it loose, like she always did. Her plan was to take the servant's daughter with her, but at the last minute she went alone. Her hand shook when she reached for the bell, and she wondered who would open the door. If it was the wife, it'd be awkward. Thankfully, Mr. Bhattarai appeared, in his hands a copper vase full of orchids.

How fitting that he should pluck the orchids for her home and she was here now, he said. He could have been lying; he had to be lying, but it didn't matter. He was afraid, though, that the quality of orchids this year wasn't as decent as last year's. She looked at the flowers and didn't notice anything lacking, but she was hardly an expert in horticulture. She didn't know he was this interested in plants—had he always been? Gardening was his hobby; it was therapeutic. Would she prefer tea or coffee? Water was good, she replied. He would ask the maid—the robot (ha-ha)—to squeeze some fruit for two glasses of juice. He especially wanted lots of lychees in his drink. Was her retirement any better? She had begun reading Mills & Boon, and it was engrossing. Her husband would hide the books soon because she didn't play cards with him. Going by the way she was, she'd soon be reading more than she did before the children came along.

She had been to his house before. In fact, she had been subject to an empty trash can flung at her by his wife in the same living room. She noticed a lot of the living room had changed. The glass-topped coffee table was missing. Furniture with sharp edges had been baby-proofed with wads of cloth held together with transparent tape. Yes, that's so Manju doesn't get hurt. Yes, so she doesn't get hurt, she repeated. She looked around to see if she'd catch a glimpse of Mrs. Bhattarai, his Manju. She could have asked him where she was, but she wasn't going to.

He suggested they go to the studio. It was not really a studio, but a part of the guest house converted into his workspace, he added. They left the house from a side door. He stopped midway to get rid of a leech on his calf by using a stray twig for the insect to climb on to. He probably attracted it when plucking the orchids. She thought of proposing they sprinkle salt on the leech to kill it, but when she saw the great care he took to ensure it would escape unharmed, she became ashamed of her thoughts and was glad she made no such suggestion. His calf was red, and she almost touched it. Mother's instinct, she justified her action. Would he need anything for it? Not a thing, please, it happened every day in the garden.

She wasn't much of an artist to judge his work. Besides a pair of paintings of Mount Kanchendzonga—one with the sun rising from its folds, another with clouds concealing a good portion of it—most of his works were portraits. Several were of his sons at various ages. Had he been painting for a while? No, he had taken up painting only in the last couple of months. He hadn't seen his older son in eight years and his younger one in six. She was afraid she'd have to wait that long—or longer—before she saw her children again. He showed her a portrait of his wife. He asked her to observe the eyes, to eliminate the eyes from the other body parts. She said the eyes alone were eerie. That's how his wife's eyes now looked—haunted and suffering, he replied.

They moved to the alcove, where she saw paintings of herself—one of her running alone, another of her walking pensively, and a third one, her favorite, of her being pulled in different directions by her dogs. Did he go around painting pictures of his fellow joggers? He once painted an old couple that lived by the peepal tree, but when he couldn't get the man's contours right, he gave up. Could she take the painting with the dogs? She would buy it even. Wouldn't her husband mind that her portrait was done by some other man? She hadn't thought of it that way. Well, now was the time to think of it. She looked at him; he looked at her. He'd now show her his best work yet—but she shouldn't mind, for he was an artist, and artists often did things unacceptable to society. Would she like to see it? Now that she was already here, why not? He unveiled a painting of a woman who looked like her suckling a grown man, who also bore a strong resemblance to her—the man's mouth obscured her breasts. Her love for her younger son inspired him to paint this "masterpiece," if you will, he said. It represented motherhood everywhere—the purest kind of love to exist. The breasts weren't shown because he didn't want the picture to be considered vulgar. She'd have to go. Wait, he shouted. He wanted her to take the orchids home. He had plucked them for her. He meant he had plucked them for her home. She said she understood what he meant and he didn't have to correct himself for the slip. She couldn't carry all the orchids. Would it be all right if the maid brought the bouquet down later? He told her the fruit juice was yet to come. She said she was in a hurry and rushed down the stairs.

The husband recounted the cards and saw the pack was only fifty-one strong.

"I think we are missing a club," he said. "The jack."

She took the pack from him and separated the cards by suits into four columns.

"No, it's here," she said, pointing at a jack of clubs. "It's something else."

"I am pretty sure we didn't have it yesterday," the husband said.

"We had it yesterday. I remember getting it way too many times."

She thought of yesterday and felt a ringing in her ears. The husband got up to look for something and came back with a fading sweetmeat box that contained a motley of cards—various colors, various patterns.

"We probably buy a pack a week," the husband said. "All right, higher to deal. Maybe we should take up a more constructive hobby, like writing or painting."

"Let's make a written list of chores." She felt her eyes lower. "You always lie that we were playing for an easier chore when I win."

"Nice, positive attitude you're beginning the session with," the husband said, in his voice a definite undercurrent of sarcasm. "Reading Mills & Boons must have done that for you."

"Peeling potatoes, refilling supplies, plucking orchids, cleaning the guest room," she said, noting them down in her curlicue writing. "In that order."

"Can't the robot pluck the orchids? Didn't we receive some from Mr. Bhattarai as it is?"

"Okay, let's replace orchids with making tea." Her legs itched.

"May the best man win," the husband said, turning a queen. "Morning shows the day."

"As childhood shows the man," the wife completed his sentence. She picked a five. "All right, you deal."

The husband was just about done dealing nine cards each when the wife's cell phone beeped somewhere.

"I have to go get that," she said.

"All right," said the husband. He smiled a sinister smile.

"Nice try—like I will leave you alone with the entire pack of cards."

"You don't have an option, do you?"

"We need to cancel this round," the wife said. "I haven't looked at my cards yet, and neither have you."

She folded her cards and ran to find her cell phone. The beeping had stopped by the time she got to it.

"It's from the US." She checked to see how many calls she had missed. "Probably Latha. She called once. No, she also called when were at breakfast."

"I am sure she'll call back again."

"Probably." The husband dealt. "We'll call her in the evening. I chatted with Sachin and Rakesh today. Both of them said your idea wasn't so bad after all."

"How come I always miss their calls?" she said. "What idea?"

"The old-age home."

"Oh, I had forgotten about it."

"Their condition was that it would have to be in America."

"You don't like traveling down to Bagdogra. I am sure an old-age home in America will suit you excellently."

"But it's America—imagine. We can brag to the Bhattarais and the Chettris about living in an old-age home in America."

You'd have to be a fool not to sense his mockery.

"And we'll reserve a plane so you can travel in peace without your long legs giving you any trouble."

"You're no fun," he joked.

"I think it's a stupid idea anyway," she said.

"What is a stupid idea?"

"Living in an old-age home."

"I nearly deposited two hundred thousand rupees in Rakesh's account, but then I thought better of it."

"What made you change your mind?"

"I smother him, you're right. He's no longer a suckling baby. We need to allow him to fly away."

"I know how you are," he said with a chuckle. "Now that you have some people agreeing with you, you don't like the idea anymore. Some suggestions you make only to get a rise out of people, don't you?"

"You know me well. After all, we've been married longer than is healthy."

"Looks like someone's had an overdose of Mills & Boon."

"I'll get rid of all of them," she said, as she shuffled the cards. "Their notion of romance is weird. I just don't get it."

The Immigrants

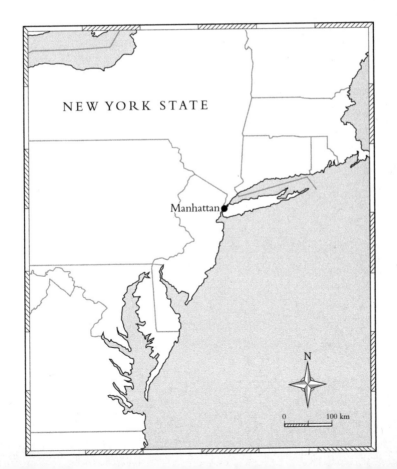

NEW YORK STATE

Manhattan

N

0   100 km

I knew I'd leave the restaurant smelling like spices. Fortunately, I had long ago learned to lessen the pungency of restaurant odors by folding my peacoat into my backpack before I set foot in any South Asian eatery. The waiter, who was also the cook, saw me come in, granted me a simulation of a smile and resumed chopping. Outside the window by my favorite seat, the rains pattered on the Manhattan streets, and a fur-coat-clad elderly woman, classically Upper East Side, caught my eye. She frantically waved for a taxi with her free hand while using the other to control her umbrella, which the wind whipped inside out.

When a particularly strong gust hurled her umbrella half-way down the block, she raised her middle finger. I'd have to help this woman—she looked fragile and well dressed, and if I stood to gain nothing from this altruistic gesture, I'd at least have spent three precious moments with a rich person, an act that always made me feel wealthy and happy. I asked the waiter-cook to prepare two plates of momos for me and, paying little heed to the pouring sky, stormed out of the restaurant to make a dash for the umbrella. The handle had become separated and was now rolling off into the traffic, so I used the rest of the umbrella to shield myself from the rain as I hastened to the soaked woman.

"Thank you so much, you kind man," the woman said, hurrying under the umbrella.

"You're welcome," I replied, displaying my most charming smile. She probably saw a set of uneven yellow teeth, an overbite, and gray dental fillings. "You won't get a cab anytime soon. Perhaps you could wait in the restaurant back there until it stops raining?"

"I don't see why not" came the unhesitant reply in a clipped accent that evoked New England. Or moneyed New York.

The woman removed her coat upon entering the restaurant, looked around for a hanger, and, finding none, placed it on a chair next to her.

"What a day," I remarked. It was raining harder.

"I am Anne," she said.

"Amen is right," I replied. At first, I mistook her introduction as an "Amen" to my account and was surprised when she extended her hand. Regaining my senses, I said, "I am Amit. What's your name?"

"I am Anne," she repeated.

"Yes, yes, Anne, you already told me that," I said, feeling like a fool. "Sorry."

"No problem, Ahmed . . . right?"

"Amit. A-M-I-T." It had happened so many times since my move to America that it no longer upset me.

We sat there staring at each other. This was awkward.

"How hungry are you?" I asked.

"Very hungry," she said. "Do you come here often?"

I did. I came to Café Himalaya a lot. Despite having been away from home for so long, I didn't have a real yearning for it, except when it came to momos, and Café Himalaya was the only place in Manhattan where you could get decent Tibetan dumplings, the closest thing to Darjeeling momos in the city. For months after moving to New York, I found a poor substitute in Chinatown dim sums—the soy sauce just didn't feel right as an accompaniment, and the flour wrapping was disappointingly thick, making the dumplings taste like an amateur attempt at my favorite food. I considered it one of my luckiest days when I walked by this café, so inconspicuously sandwiched between a bar and a Thai restaurant that I would never have noticed it had the larger-than-life portrait of the Dalai Lama on one of its walls not aroused my curiosity. I had returned at least twice a week ever since.

"My favorite is the chicken momo," I said, pointing at its description on the menu. "I usually eat two plates of them— they are so good. I've already ordered."

"Oh, momos," Anne remarked in delight. "I just ate them last week."

This was interesting. It's not every day that you came across an American who knew about momos. When I told people I was of Nepalese origin, they instinctively asked me if I had climbed Mount Everest. When I answered no, I hadn't climbed Everest and no, I did not know anyone who had, they were disappointed. When I mentioned I was from Darjeeling, most people asked me a tea question. When I let them know I couldn't distinguish one variety from another and that I didn't drink tea, they looked bewildered. And if I told anyone I was an Indian with Nepalese origins, they looked at me in wide-eyed wonder, sometimes pressing me to volunteer information about this curious mishmash. I wouldn't have minded recounting my family history so much if the inevitable "So, you're half-Nepalese and half-Indian?" question didn't come up. Sometimes I drew a map and went through a spiel on the difference between ethnicity and nationality. Most other times, I just stayed silent and let people continue living in their uninformed bubbles.

"How do you know about them?" I asked, unable to hide my excitement.

"Are you a Nepali?"

"Yes, I am," I said. "A Nepali from India."

"Yes, yes, there are a lot of you in India, right? Himachal?"

"No, Darjeeling."

"Beautiful, beautiful place." She looked outside. Two teenagers jumped into the slush, drenching passersby.

"Have you been?" I asked.

"These rains must remind you of the place."

"Yes, it rains a lot. And we get landslides, but it doesn't rain this way in March. It's still very cold."

"It's cold in New York. It will be cold until the middle of April."

"So, have you been to Darjeeling?" I asked again. The rains came down like they did in Darjeeling, something that smelled like home spluttered in the kitchen, and the momos would soon be here. A little conversation about all the places in Darjeeling Anne might have visited—the Chowrasta, Glenary's, the zoo, and the Ghoom Monastery—would be an excellent way to end this dreary day.

"No, I haven't," she said.

I paused, waiting for her to qualify her answer, but she had nothing to add. I was with the worst conversationalist in the world.

"You seem familiar with it."

"I am sorry. I was just thinking of someone. No, I haven't been to Darjeeling, but I have a maid who is Nepali. I was just reminded of her. She began working for me recently. She makes good momos. I also read about different places."

She brought the chopsticks down on a momo and put the entire thing in her mouth, looking like a masticating beast.

"She's a nice girl." She continued swallowing the dumpling. "Her language is still poor, but she understands me well and gets along well with my grandkids. I'll tell her I met you."

"Does she live with you?" I asked.

"No, she lives in Queens. Not Jackson Heights. The other neighborhood."

"I am not very familiar with Queens," I boasted. I was hoping she'd ask where I lived, but she didn't.

She thought hard. "Sunnyside? No. Woodside, Woodside." She was on her third momo by now. "These are good. The inside isn't so spicy. I like them better."

"Yes, we Darjeeling people eat momos slightly different from the ones in Nepal. Our insides are bland. All the spices are in the chutney."

"I don't like the chutney." She pronounced it *choot-ney.* "Gives me heartburn."

"So this girl—your maid—is she from Kathmandu?"

"Yes, but originally from a village in the hills. She's a nice girl, but communication sometimes is a problem. She's great at what she does."

"Does she come every day?"

"She's off Saturdays and Tuesdays. I tell her she doesn't have to cook, but she likes the kitchen. And she sometimes makes good stuff. By now she knows I don't like spices so much. I like the way they smell, though—raw and fresh."

Yes, the spices that stink up your apartment, and your clothes and your hair. I didn't want to think of how long the smell of spices from this restaurant would linger on my clothes. No precaution was good enough.

"My maid comes in about twice a week," I lied. She came every two weeks. "She's very good, but I've always wanted a South Asian maid. I am tired of eating all my three—well, I skip breakfast—meals out. It'd be excellent if someone came in once a week or so and made enough food to last me a couple of days. I'd just need to boil the rice."

I hoped this scrap of information would impress her. It stunned everyone I met when I said I had a maid. It was like mentioning my Manhattan apartment, the one I owned and did not rent. Sure, it may have been in the middle of Harlem, the part still not associated with gentrification and urban renewal, and the entire place was the size of my room in Darjeeling. But it was in a nice building, and I knew it was a solid investment.

"Wait, you should hire Sabitri," Anne said. Clearly, nothing would enthrall this millionaire—neither a twenty-five-year-old owning a piece of Manhattan nor a twenty-five-year-old having a maid. "She keeps trying to tell me she wants more work. None of my friends want to hire her because of language issues. The poor thing has been in America five years, but her English has shown little improvement. She could come to your place on her days off. Maybe you could teach her English."

I had never looked for a Nepalese maid. I liked my German maid fine. A Pakistani friend and I joked in college about how a brown man's biggest aspiration was to hire white help. Honestly, I was only half joking then; to me, having a white maid was an indication that I had made it. Letting the world know that I had a German maid made me feel smug and superior, not that I would ever admit it to anyone but the Pakistani. It made me feel like I had climbed yet another ladder of success. There you go, Baba, I thought, wasn't it you who discouraged me from going to America and warned I'd have to wash dishes here? All these white people's dishes? This is what I get, Aamaa, when I dream bigger than being an instructor at a college in Darjeeling. Well, here I was, with an apartment and a maid in New York—a white German maid, whom I had no intention of ever getting rid of. The idea of eating home-cooked food every day, however, appealed to me.

"Is she very expensive?" I asked, finishing my momo. A plate was just not enough these days. "I do not want to fire my current maid. I'd have to accommodate both of them."

"She charges me seventy dollars a day," Anne said, blowing ripples on the tea that our unsmiling waiter-cook generously provided us with today. "She needs to subsidize her rate if she wants some English lessons from you."

"No, no, it's not the money," I said. "But is she as good as you say she is?"

"Take my word for it. She's excellent."

"Can you give her my number?" I handed her my card.

The downpour had calmed into a drizzle. The check arrived, and I offered to pay. To my surprise, Anne accepted.

"Do you want to split a cab home?" I asked.

"Where do you live?"

"I just bought an apartment close to Riverside Drive." I grabbed the opportunity. My apartment was half a dozen blocks away from Riverside Drive, and the area was nothing as nice.

"I live in Gramercy," she said as we stepped outside. "You'll probably want to take a different one."

A cab pulled up. I retrieved my coat from my backpack.

"Thanks again for the umbrella and the momos," she said, not ungraciously. "I'll make sure Sabitri gives you a call."

To some people, owning a Manhattan apartment in your early twenties with zero help from your parents is just not extraordinary enough.

Sabitri called me at work the next day. I wasn't at my desk because my boss and I were meeting with the human resources director to iron out the details of my application for the H-1B, the visa that would entitle me to work legally in America for another three years. On the expiration of the three-year term, I could get the visa extended for another three, after which I would be eligible for a green card. I had my future in America all mapped out and was excited about the next big step.

The morning's meeting was tedious, but I had been success-ful in getting the company to pay for the sponsorship, a notion my boss was initially opposed to. Wanting to share the big news with somebody—anybody—I picked up the phone but didn't know whom to call and instead checked my voice mail. A few seconds of static later, a voice said "Hello," followed it with "*Chee hou*" and a nervous laugh. It had to be Sabitri. I called her back.

"This is Amit," I said in English. "Anne must have told you to call me."

"Oh, Madam." She switched to Nepali. "Yes, I called you today. I didn't know she had given you my number, too."

"No, no," I said and then adjusted to Nepali. "I got the number from my phone. She says you're interested in English lessons."

"Yes, where in Nepal are you from?" she asked. "Madam told me about meeting a Nepali from India. I was a bit confused." She spoke the kind of antiquated Nepali we in Darjeeling made fun of and associated with poor villagers—her verbs agreed with the gender as well as the status of her subjects, a concept we grasped with great difficulty in school and never really used outside the academic world.

"I am from India. Darjeeling. Where are you from?"

"I am originally from Rolpa, but my parents have moved to Jamunaa, near Ilam. Have you been there?"

"No, I have never been to Nepal."

"You haven't been to your own country?" She was genuinely shocked.

"My country is India. I've always wanted to go to Nepal, but I've never been there."

"Then how come you speak such excellent Nepali?"

"Everyone in Darjeeling speaks Nepali. We speak Nepali at home. I am Nepali."

"But for a Nepali your Nepali is really bad," she pointed out.

"We speak a different Nepali from the Nepali you people in Nepal do."

She didn't pursue the topic.

"Madam tells me you want someone to cook Nepali food. I can do that. I am free Saturdays and Tuesdays." She used the Nepali names for the days. No one I knew besides my grandmother did that. In Darjeeling, we—at least people my generation—peppered our Nepali with English words.

"What are those days in English?"

She let me know.

"Should we start this week?" she asked. It was Thursday. This strange woman, this pushy Nepalese, was ready to be at my place Saturday. Soon, I would walk into work smelling like I had been doused in turmeric. And we hadn't even brought up payment.

"How much money are we talking?" I asked.

"Why should there be money involved?" Her tone was defensive. "It's one Nepali helping another. I cook your food, and you teach me English. Problem solved. Let's not be petty."

Her feistiness was as alarming as her use of big Nepali words.

These were not the only aspects of her personality that would surprise me. She also had no respect for my time. Early Saturday morning, I received a call from her asking me what time we were supposed to meet.

"Wasn't it two?" I asked, looking at the alarm clock and resisting the temptation to break it.

"Two? I can come by earlier if you want. I could clean a bit, too."

"But I've another maid to clean my place," I said.

An uncomfortable silence greeted me. *Kaam garne* in Nepali is definitely more euphemistic than "maid" and crudely translates to "servant," an undignified but still widely used term, and I had just categorized her as one.

"You know, she does my laundry and cleans the toilet." I hoped I wasn't worsening the situation. "I wouldn't expect you to do all that. It wouldn't be right. I wouldn't feel right. But if you want to come early, please feel free. I just woke up. It will take you an hour to get here."

"I can be there in half an hour," she said.

By the time I buzzed her in, I was showered and shaved.

"Hello." A plain-looking girl, clad in inexpensive jeans and a *kurti*, with a nose too pronounced, greeted me. You would have dismissed her appearance back home as ordinary but found her attractive after a few years in America influenced you to change your standards of beauty. "*Ammamama,* lots of *hapshis* in this area."

"It's Harlem," I said. "This was once the capital of Black America, so, yes, you will find lots of black people. But it's changing. A lot of young professionals have moved in. I bought this place only two months ago, but a lot of people like me are moving in."

"Bought?"

"Yes." I tried not to sound too proud.

"It must be expensive."

"It's all right."

"I haven't come across any Nepali who owns property." She placed her purse on the coffee table. "Not in Woodside. Not in Jackson Heights. Not in Manhattan, obviously."

"A lot of them own their places, I am sure, and I am an Indian. How long have you lived here?"

"It's been a little over five years." She looked around at my apartment.

"Did you—" I had difficulty framing the question—"first come on a tourist visa?" This insinuated that she was an illegal immigrant, one of those thousands who arrive in this country on a tourist visa but never leave.

"No, I am a citizen now," she replied, her eyes once again scanning the apartment. "I won the DV lottery."

Okay, she was a diversity-visa winner. I had always been jealous of her kind. America, in an attempt to boost diversity, offered a program that allowed people of underrepresented nations to enter a draw. Those who got lucky, such as Sabitri, received their green cards while we ordinary mortals needed to jump through countless hoops before getting one. But didn't one need to pass an English test to be a citizen? If Sabitri had problems with her language, as Anne mentioned, the most lenient interviewer must have tested her on the citizenship exam.

"Lucky," I said. "People would give their children's lives to win one."

"That's what they say in Nepal," she said. "But I am working as a *kaam garne* here. No one in my family knows it."

"No one in the family knows it?" I repeated. Her choice of words to describe her job threw me off.

"They think I am working in an office. And no one knows about the seven people who are my roommates. Three are men. Almost all of them are illegal."

As someone familiar with the reality of poverty in India, and South Asia for that matter, I knew that seven people crowding into one-bedroom apartments wasn't such an issue. I attempted to frame a sentence in my mind to let her know in the least offensive way that I understood, when she spoke.

"The kitchen's slightly small, but this is a nice place," she said.

Again, she used the Nepali term for "kitchen," a word I had long forgotten. Had she not been staring at the kitchen when she described it, I wouldn't have guessed what she was talking about.

"Seven people living in a one-bedroom apartment isn't so bad, is it? I am sure it's bigger than this."

She sized up my apartment.

"Yes, it is bigger but not so nice. Most of these people didn't have much money in Nepal, so to them our place is great. I don't like it, but I shouldn't complain. Wouldn't people give up their children to be here?" She smiled. Her teeth were better than mine, though her smile hardly lit her face.

"How is working with Anne?" I asked.

"She's nice, really nice, but I know I'll die if I stay there forever," she replied. "There's nothing to do. Americans are clean people. Sometimes her grandchildren visit, but they are very disciplined kids. The granddaughter wants me to teach her a Nepali dance. I don't even know how to dance so well."

It didn't escape my notice that she was avoiding a pronoun to summon me. The Nepali language has three variations of the second-person pronoun, dependent mostly on respect, age, intimacy, and familiarity. I addressed her with the same pronoun I used for elders. It sounded contrived, and she was clearly uncomfortable.

"Something to drink?" I asked, the absurdity of the question not failing me—here was a prospective maid being asked if she wanted anything by her employer. It'd have been unthinkable were we back home.

"I'll make something," she said. "Coffee?"

Of course, the kitchen had no coffee, and the fridge was empty. I asked her if she wanted me to accompany her to the grocery store, a proposition she was only too happy about.

"It will give me an idea of what to buy in the future," she said.

We wandered along the aisles of the supermarket scouring for the staples of South Asian cooking—rice, lentils, chickpeas, cloves, nutmeg, and spices whose anglicized names I had never known—before returning home. While waiting in the checkout line, Sabitri leaned over to whisper about her discomfort with blacks after spotting a dark-skinned man ahead of us. It was a strangely intimate thing to do and, taken aback as I was, I tried not to think too much of it. She hadn't been assimilated well enough, and derogatory comments based on skin color were hardly uncommon among people back home. I couldn't hold her to American standards of political correctness just yet.

I would have helped her put the groceries away on our return, but the kitchen was too small for both of us to be working together without bumping into each other.

"I'll watch TV," I said. "Let me know if you need anything."

"All right," she replied.

I had forgotten to tell her to go light on the spices but decided not to until I had smelled and tasted her food. The kitchen area bustled with activity—the never-used pressure cooker whistled and the blender ground—as she hummed Bollywood numbers in synchrony with the clattering pots. I smiled to myself and tried concentrating on the *Full House* rerun on TV, not annoyed by the intrusion from the kitchen. The apartment was soon really hot—that's what cooking in a shoebox, even if it's March, can do—and I asked Sabitri if she wanted me to turn the air conditioner on. She replied she didn't mind because she was used to living without the convenience.

Soon a variety of aromas filled the apartment. Curious, I entered the kitchen. Half a dozen Tupperware containers, filled to the brim with daal, sautéed spinach, and potato curry, were ready to be deposited into the freezer. Sabitri labeled which container held what with Post-it notes in Nepali. Yellow dominated the countertops, the dishes, and the floor, and a combination of odors from Darjeeling and Café Himalaya piqued my nostrils as she rationed out my food for the rest of the week before setting the table for me.

"What about your plate?" I asked.

"I'll eat later."

"No, you can eat with me."

She took a plate and sat in the dining chair farthest from me.

"What do your parents do?"

I had complimented her on the food, which, though not excellent, I still liked. I have always maintained that Nepalese cooking has become infiltrated by the growing influence of

North Indian cuisine. The usage of spices, grease, and oil in Nepalese food is these days bordering on the excessive, robbing the cuisine of its authenticity, and making it North Indian–like. The meal Sabitri prepared was just Nepali enough, and it wouldn't cause me the digestive damage that meals from Indian restaurants often did. I could sacrifice finger-licking delicious for healthy and agreeable on the constitution.

"My father is a clerk, and my mother's a housewife," she said. It was jarring how few English words crept into her speech despite her five years in America.

"And how many brothers and sisters do you have?"

"A younger brother. He's in Class Eight. Failed last year."

"Does he study in Kathmandu?"

"No, he's in Ilam with my uncle. Mount Mechi." It was a tone that expected me to be familiar with the school. I nodded.

"So, are you sending money home?" Often, when you're dealing with people below you in class, the most personal questions aren't deemed as inappropriate. I asked every cabbie I came across how much he made.

"Yes, I am." She got up to go to the kitchen. "I've been sending it since the first month I got here. We had to take out a loan for my airfare and my first month's rent."

That was news to me. While I didn't exactly grow up with a silver spoon in my mouth—my parents were both lecturers at North Point College—I didn't know anyone who had to get a loan to come to America.

"How do we want to do the English lessons?" she asked from the kitchen.

Until then, I hadn't really given the lessons much thought.

"Sabitri." She looked me in the eye—it was the first time I had called her by her name and also the first time we stared at each other that long. "From now on, we'll always, always, always speak in English."

* / * / *

It was awkward at first. When she returned Tuesday evening, I could see she was hoping I had forgotten about only speaking in English. The minute she opened her mouth, I said, in English, "I am sure what you are about to say is in English."

I spoke slowly and softly, enunciating words with more than three syllables and ensuring that my sentences had fewer than ten words.

"How was your day?" I started. In English.

"Fine."

"Could you tell me something about it?"

"Sorry."

"Tell me something about your day." Measured, six words.

"I wake up." Pause. "I waked up, I ate my foods, and then washing clothes, cleaning house, and then I cook lunch. I came here."

"How did you come here?"

"Subway."

"Subway—what?" I said.

She looked at me, unsure. "I took subway to come here."

"Did you not go to Anne's today?"

"No. Today holiday."

This exhausted me. I was never good at small talk. And this was like small talk with a child. I'd have to spice it up.

"How many members are there in your family?"

"Four."

"Who are they, and how old are they?"

"My father—his name Purna Bahadur Karki. He is fifty-four. My mother is forty. Benimaya Karki. My brother is Samik Karki. Sixteen year old."

"What does your father do?"

"He is clerk in office."

"Does he make good money?"

"No, my family very poor. I send them money every month."

"Do you miss your family?"

"No. I like it here."

"What about your roommates?"

"Some of them smells." She covered her nose. "All poor people, even poorer than me."

"Who's your best friend?"

"I like Binita, but lazy."

"Why do you say so?"

"See don't want to learn how to use the computer. And see pass high school." Like many Nepali-speaking people, she couldn't properly pronounce words like "she" and "shower."

"What about you?"

"I pass high school, too, and I learn how to use the computer from Dev."

"Who's Dev?"

"My another roommate."

"How does he know how to use the computer?"

"He learn in Kathmandu."

"What do you do on the computer?"

"I watched YouTube videos in computer."

"Can you send e-mails?"

"Yes."

"From now on, you will send me e-mails."

"Yes."

"One paragraph on what you did that day. Every day."

"Yes."

"Do you like your work?"

"I earn better than friends."

"What's your ambition?"

"Sorry."

"Am-bi-tion?"

She shook her head. "Sorry?"

"Am-bee-shun—what do you want to become in life? A teacher, a doctor, a pilot?"

"Don't know. Make a lots of money."

"How?"

"Own store one day."

"What kind of a store?"

"Clothes store."

"Cool," I said.

We developed a pattern.

Tuesdays, we'd ride the subway uptown together from my workplace. She started cooking right away while I changed in the bedroom and shouted conversation with her. We spoke only in English. While something marinated in the kitchen, we went through printouts of her e-mails; I pointed out mistakes or praised her for an error-free sentence. She was a fast learner and seldom repeated errors. When she did, she rebuked herself by hitting her forehead a couple of times. As she garnished or ladled out food in the kitchen, I pulled a chair close by and engaged her in a translation game in which she had to come up with an English word for every Nepali noun I mentioned. The tight space was disconcerting at first, and I still placed the chair as far away from her as I could, but it was a tiny kitchen. She needed to move a lot, and her ponytail occasionally brushed against my shoulders when she energetically turned her head to translate a word I threw at her.

Saturdays, she came in early in the morning. I had discovered the beauty and freshness of farmers' markets when I was in school back in Pennsylvania, but I hadn't been to one in New York. With Sabitri's arrival early in the morning and my awaking well before the usual time as a result, a farmers' market was the best place to go. Every Saturday, long before eight, we stood in line for the freshest produce in Manhattan and returned home with enough food to feed an orphanage. I helped Sabitri put away the groceries, after which she cooked while I did laundry or cleaned—she had convinced me to get rid of my German maid. The slow, labored conversation continued throughout the day. I had asked her to begin thinking in English. In the beginning, she said it was impossible to stop thinking in a language spoken since birth. She'd soon begin dreaming in English if I repeated myself often enough, I reasoned.

Back issues of *New York* and *The New Yorker* littered my bathroom floor, and one day she asked me what the magazines were doing there.

"I read in the bathroom," I said.

"I don't believed you," she remarked.

"Yes, I do. It's the most productive thing to do."

"But I don't knows anyone who does that." She was incredulous.

"I do, and a lot of people I know do that."

"*Chee*," she offered by way of disapproval.

"You just used a Nepali word." I gave her a stern look.

"But only one, and it's not word even."

"You could use the English word for it. It's 'eww.'"

"Ewwww?"

"Yes."

"Anne grandchildrens says that when I show them how to eat a chicken with hands."

"Did they?" This was funny. "So now you know *chee* is 'eww.'"

"Yes, ewwww." She repeated it a few times and laughed. Soon, she was in convulsions. "Eww, eww."

"What's so funny?"

"I think, I thinks . . ." she struggled to find the right words and laughed again.

"Yes, tell me."

"Can I say in Nepali? Too hard—tough, really hard."

"No, English, English." I was stubborn.

She began saying a word, shook her head vigorously, tried reconstructing the sentence, lost track midway and started all over again. I was sympathetic, and yet I began to lose patience. "Okay, one last chance in Nepali."

It was nothing. When she demonstrated to Anne's grandchildren the art of picking shreds of chicken from the bones, the way her family in Nepal did toward the end of their meals, she misunderstood their disgust for enthusiasm. It was only now that she realized they weren't encouraging her to continue slurping and sucking on her chicken bones but to stop it. The memory of it prompted her to slap my thigh as she shook with laughter.

Saturday evenings, we went to Central Park, where I encouraged her to speak to everyone. She asked for directions, talked to children, and behaved like a clueless tourist. When someone understood her on the first go, she gave me a jubilant look and skipped happily. Sometimes children, especially, didn't understand her even after she repeated herself. She then hit herself on the forehead a few times, cursed her stupidity in Nepali, and asked me what was wrong with the question she framed. Often, it was just the diction and the tone, but she was convinced of a bigger problem.

With my German maid gone, Sabitri did the dishes, the mopping, and dusting and also helped with the laundry. I wouldn't allow her to clean the bathroom, and I think she was thankful for that. To her, it meant I respected her, that I thought the job wasn't dignified enough for her although it wasn't beneath me. She had a key to the apartment and when nothing happened at Anne's, which was often, she let herself into my place and spruced it up or cooked an unexpected meal, which greeted me with a Post-it note—in English—mentioning what it was. Smiley faces abounded.

* * *

May brought with it a problem in an envelope. My office received a returned letter containing the check it sent to the United States Citizenship and Immigration Services. When I called a Pakistani acquaintance from college, he told me his check had been returned, too. We were among the people whose H-1B visa applications had been turned down. Because the number of applicants that year had far exceeded the number of visas allotted, the USCIS had adopted a lottery system, just like the year before. It made no sense at all. I was a homeowner in Manhattan with a six-figure salary, and I was rejected. It was a cruel joke, a nasty game played by fate. I talked about it with my colleagues and tried crying in the bathroom. I even considered calling my parents in Darjeeling. My boss and the human resources director asked me if they might be able to help, but I knew they could do nothing. Just an hour ago, the Pakistani friend let me know that the petition of one of his friends who graduated from Yale had been rejected. There was nothing he— or I—could do.

My flawlessly laid plans had been derailed. I was aware of what went on in those IT offices in Jersey. Of fake résumés, doctored degrees, and H-1B commissions. I was aware of at least two companies that applied for H-1Bs for people who weren't even going to be employed there. I heard and read about the semi-legal industry this H-1B craze had given birth to. Were the USCIS to probe into it all, America would realize how easily it has been taken for a ride. Salaries had been concocted, positions recreated, and numbers reinvented. It was a mutually beneficial relationship between conglomerates desperate for labor at subsidized rates and South Asians anxious for a shot at a green card and the American dream. Because everyone is too busy worrying about illegal immigrants, the issue never made its way into newspaper headlines. The people who lost out were people like me, people who had played by the book and actually deserved an H-1B.

I talked to my boss about continuing the job until the end of December, when my OPT, which facilitated my current year-long employment, would expire. I could then either go to graduate school or leave the country. I couldn't possibly keep up with my mortgage payments if I went back to college. I had used all the money I had saved since my freshman year to buy the apartment. Leaving the country meant returning home without having accomplished a thing. I thought of calling Sabitri, but the idea of having to explain everything to her as if she were a child while my mind raced at an unfathomable speed dissuaded me from it.

The next Tuesday, on our ride uptown, Sabitri asked me what the matter was.

"Nothing," I said.

"It is something."

"Can I speak to you in Nepali?"

"No," she said in shock. She was perhaps offended at the idea that I thought she wouldn't understand me.

"Okay. I'll tell you."

"Yes, I am listening."

"My H-1B visa got turned down."

She was quiet.

"My work visa got rejected." I hoped she wouldn't catch the ballooning lump in my throat. The last time I cried was eleven years ago.

"What's the problem?"

"I can only legally work until the end of December."

"What will you do after that?"

"I'll probably have to leave the country, go back home."

"You mean Nepal?" She still hadn't made peace with the fact that I was from India.

"Yes, India."

"Any more options you have?"

"Graduate school."

"That's better."

"But I need to pay my mortgage."

"You can do that. You can get job in school."

"That may not happen. I need to get into a school in New York if I want to continue living in my apartment."

"What if you get roommate?"

"You've seen how small my apartment is. Who would want to live there? Even a full-sized bed barely fits in my bedroom."

"You can put advertisement for it."

"It won't work."

"You're being—" she stuttered—"pessi-pessimitic now."

Despite what I felt like, I had to smile. This was a heroic effort, a decent word for someone who barely knew English.

"Pessimistic," I corrected.

"Oh, yes," she said, hitting her forehead.

"But it's a great word. And you used it correctly."

"But pronounce it wrongly."

"I still think it's great you used it."

"Okay, now be optimistic." She smiled. She was full of surprises today.

"I am trying to. It's just that my plans went out the window."

"I thought I will go to Ratna Rajya College for my BBA. I am servant now."

"This is different."

"How different? It's the same."

She used an article, goddamnit. "You moved to better things. I am moving to worse."

"Better things? I am wiping shit of Madam's grandchildren. This is not better things."

"I don't want to go to grad school."

"Grad school is better things."

"How will I afford it?"

"By savings."

"Like that's possible."

"It is. If you start now."

"Ugh, I need to find a roommate. I will have to sleep on the couch now."

"I think I know of roommate for you." Wow, she *was* full of surprises today.

"Who?"

"Is it problem if it is girl?"

"No, not at all."

"Me." She corrected herself. "I mean I, myself."

Sabitri moved in two days later. She repeatedly told me that she chose to live with me not so she could help me with the mortgage payments but because her male roommates were drunk every night, making her and her female friends uncomfortable. This was like it was meant to happen, she added. A suitcase, half of it filled with English textbooks, was the lone item she brought. She took the closet by the kitchen despite my repeatedly telling her that her clothes would reek with kitchen smells. I insisted that she take my bed and that I would sleep on the couch, but she wouldn't have any of that. If she was unyielding, so was I, and I slept on the bare hardwood floor. When I peeped into the living room, I saw her sleeping on the floor, too. The couch and the bed lay empty.

I heard her turning—the floor creaked—and asked her if she was asleep.

"I fell asleep if I sleep in something comfortable," came the answer.

"Then take the bed."

"No."

"Fine, then sleep on the couch."

Silence.

"We both know we will not fall asleep on the floor."

"Okay, I will sleep on couch, but you sleep on bed."

"All right, I will do that."

She climbed on the couch.

"It folds out," I said.

She didn't reply. It was our first argument.

The next morning, she brought me tea while I was still in bed.

"You don't have to do all this," I said in Nepali. It sounded awkward even to me.

"I made tea for myself," she said, a smile acknowledging my slipping into Nepali. "No extra work make it for you."

"But even then. I am not paying you for it."

"But look how much my English improved. From now, you teach me all English, and I do all housework. Groceries and rent fifty-fifty."

I didn't know if it was the finality with which she said the last sentence or the sight of her bare legs that unsettled me. Until then, I had only seen her in pants or skirts, but this morning, she still wore the shorts she slept in. The discomfort likely showed, for she avoided my gaze and quickly left the bedroom.

We developed a new routine. She brought me coffee in bed, I headed to the shower, we ate breakfast, left home together, I got off at Midtown, she went to Gramercy, she was usually home before I was, and we ate dinner together. We talked about our days, and I'd study for the GRE while she read. I was successful in getting a friend from Darjeeling to courier us some of my old Enid Blyton *Noddy* books. She went through them cover to cover, read and reread them. When I was bored of studying and lingered in front of the TV too long, she switched it off, placed her hands on the back of my shoulders, as if she were pushing an immobile car, and steered me into the bedroom. She had found a job for Saturdays and Tuesdays, taking one of Anne's elderly friends on long walks. She didn't mind sacrificing her days off. To her, it was easy money and a chance to work on her English, which showed decent progress.

We argued, too. She wanted the books out of the bathroom. I didn't. She said I could take whatever book I was reading and bring it back with me. That way, my magazines and newspapers wouldn't clutter the floor. I told her I'd try, and she looked victorious.

"Finally, you take maid's advice," she said.

"You don't have to refer to yourself as that. You're a friend."

"No, no, I am maid—once maid, always maid," she sang in an off-key voice.

"You're not a maid. You're friend." These days, I sometimes ignored my articles, too.

"No, maid," she argued.

"Stop it, stop it, goddamnit," I screamed. The intensity astonished me.

Her eyes grew bigger, and I could see the fear in them. I had never seen that look before.

I couldn't sleep very well that night. I knew she wasn't doing so well either. Should I have apologized? But it was she who kept ranting about being a maid. She was a maid, sure, but she was so much more than that. And what was she if not a maid? My head was heavy with thoughts, and when four Tylenols and every possible sleeping position didn't help, I staggered to the bathroom with a random book, hoping it'd distract me.

The light was already on, and crouched on the commode, reading a book, was Sabitri.

"Sorry." I closed the door and went back out into the narrow hallway. "I didn't know you were here."

"I didn't want to disturb you by put the light in living room on. I will be right out."

She came into the living room wiping her hands on her shirt. "So you're reading in the bathroom now?" I tried smiling.

"I do that from long time back."

"But you made fun of me."

"And you yell at me," she retorted.

"It's your fault."

"No."

"You are not a maid."

"You are IT professional; I am maid. It's simple."

"I am sorry I screamed at you."

"It's fine. It's okay. Don't do again."

"I won't." My voice was soft.

"Thanks. Screaming is scary."

"I know. I am sorry. Are we fine now?"

"I don't know."

"You read in the bathroom?" I chuckled.

"You teach—taught me."

"I am a great teacher."

"A good teacher never yell at his student."

"See, you are not my maid. You are my student."

"Okay, I agree. I am student."

Once we had established what she was in relation to me, Sabitri brightened up and told me about her early-morning phone call with her parents. She seldom spoke to them, and her conversations always involved money. Sometimes the parents were happy, and often they were dissatisfied. They had begun building a house—a cement house, she said—and depended on her to finance it. She wasn't bitter about it, but she wasn't too happy either. She said she made all that money—more money than her father could ever dream of—so she should help them out, especially because she lived in a gorgeous apartment and had such an easy life. When the demands for money kept increasing, she told her mother she'd send them a fixed amount of $500 every month. They'd have to budget accordingly. I seethed at their selfishness but stayed silent, which was strange because I didn't keep a whole lot to myself these days. When Columbia rejected me a few weeks later, for instance, I didn't hesitate to tell her about it.

"I am not depressed, because I knew I wasn't good enough," I said, switching on the TV.

"Promise me you will not be angry," she interrupted.

"No, I won't." I turned the TV off. "I promise."

"I am still afraid you will be getting angry."

"I promise I won't."

"First, I think I will take GED."

I was amazed. I couldn't have been prouder. She was taking the American high school equivalency exam. That she even knew about it astounded me.

"Wow, you will do very well. I am so happy."

"But that's not the main issue."

She was about ready for the GED. With her diligence, she could prepare for anything. "What's it?" I asked.

"You didn't get Columbia."

"No, I didn't get into it."

"So what? Will you go home?"

"I guess. Let me hear back from NYU, although I don't know if I will be accepted. It's almost as tough as Columbia."

"I talked to a lawyer about this," she said.

Wow, she had a lawyer, I thought, and repeated it aloud.

"Yes, Anne's son is a lawyer. His friend is an immigration lawyer."

The articles in her speech sounded beautiful.

"What did he say?"

"You promise you won't be getting angry?"

"No."

"Okay, first listen to what I am going to say."

"All right."

"Do not interrupt me." Another commendable word. I was a good teacher.

"Shoot," I said.

She cleared her throat. "I know I am only servant." She raised her hand when she saw I was about to say something. "I don't even belong same kind of family as you do. And I am your servant only. No one will have to know. I am citizen of America. You need to stay in country legally. You can marry me. It won't be real. No one has to know." She was nervous now and didn't look at me. "And after marry, you can continue your job. We can get divorce in no time. Please don't be getting angry at me."

"You're not a servant," I said. "You've never been a servant. You're not even my student. You and I—what we have is different. You're the only reason I am here today. I'd probably have given up a long time ago and returned to Darjeeling had it not been for you. You will never, never, never call yourself a servant, promise me that."

She sat there, unmoving.

"I would be lying to you if I said how many times the thought didn't occur to me," I said. "It came to me every day and every night, but I have too much respect for you to broach it. I thought it would anger you, that you'd think I took this relationship for granted, so I didn't bring it up."

"You should have brought it up."

"And spoil this great thing I have with you?"

"And what thing do we have, Amit?" It was the first time she had used my name.

"We know it's special, it's different, so why mess it up?" This sucked the life out of me. We aren't a very vocal race, and I've never been comfortable with talking about feelings.

"You're angry, are you?"

"I'm not. I just think I shouldn't marry you just so I can stay in the country. We will get married when I get a green card on my own account. I'll marry you because you're the one person I want to get married to."

"It's because I am servant, I know. You don't have to be married to me in real."

She began to cry. I let her.

Glossary of Foreign Words

Words may have alternative meanings. Each word has been translated in the context used in the book.

THE CLEFT

Aamaa: mother
aatmaa: spirit
adivasi: indigenous people
arrey: Oh!
Baba: father
bajiyaa: rascal
Bhaanjaa: nephew
Bhauju: sister-in-law; a brother's wife
bokshee: witch
chiwda: beaten rice
chyaa: expression of disgust
Daai: brother
darji: tailor
dera: rented place
dhaarey: fattened-up head louse
gori: a white woman

halla-gulla: hustle-bustle
harey: exclamation conveying frustration or surprise
Hulas: Nepalese cigarette brand
jumraa: head louse
jwaai: brother-in-law
kaam: thirteenth day purification rite; takes place thirteen days after a person's death
keti: girl
khaini: tobacco
khanchuwee: glutton
khasi: goat meat
kuiree: white woman
maiyya: sister-in-law
pagli: mad
potey: necklace worn by married women
saasu-buhaari: mother-in-law/daughter-in-law
shlokas: hymns
sindoor: vermilion powder worn on a married woman's hair parting
sishnu: nettle leaves
Teez: festival observed by Hindu women for the wellness of their husbands
Tihaar: festival of lights; also known as Diwali
tole: neighborhood
tutey-futey: broken
Yeshu: Jesus

LET SLEEPING DOGS LIE

baandar: monkey
Bahini: sister
beedi: cigarette
Chui-Mui: tiny teddy bear that became popular after being featured in an Indian song called *Chui-Mui*

Dashain: Hindu festival celebrating the victory of good over evil
Eid: Muslim festival
haathi: elephant
kukkur: dog
lakhs: a lakh is a hundred thousand (rupees in this case)
meetha paan: betel leaf not coated with tobacco
Memsaab: Ma'am
Musalmaan: Muslim person
naani: child
Namaste: greeting by bringing the hands together
oooof: expression of dismissal
paan: betel leaf
paanwalla: shopkeeper
tamasha: spectacle
zardaa paan: betel leaf coated with tobacco

A FATHER'S JOURNEY

abbui: an expression of fear
arabpatis: billionaires
Baahun: Brahmin
Battis Mile: 32nd mile, a town near Gangtok
chulhai nimto: invitation for the entire family
chyaa: expression of disgust
crorepatis: millionaires
Femina: a women's magazine
gundagiri: hooliganism
hajaarpattis: people worth thousands of rupees
Jaisi: Brahmin sub-caste
janaai: sacred thread
jwaai saab: son-in-law
Kaiyas: *Kaiya* (singular) is a derogatory, if widely used, term for
     a businessman of Indian origin
kundalis: horoscopes

kurta: loose-fitting shirt
Laal Bazaar: the farmers' market in Gangtok
laddoos: ball-shaped sweets made of flour and sugar
lakhapatis: people worth lakhs (a lakh is a hundred thousand)
    of rupees
lobhi: miserly
Matwalis: castes that incorporate drinking in their rituals
Rakhi: sacred thread sisters tie around their brothers' wrists.
    Sometimes, the Rakhi is used to establish fictive kinship
    (i.e. Rakhi brothers and sisters)

MISSED BLESSING

adda: place of assembly
bekaamey: useless
burfee: Indian sweetmeat
chema: aunt; mother's younger sister
Dashain: Hindu festival that celebrates the victory of good over evil
khadas: silk scarves
kinema: fermented soya
mama: uncle; mother's brother
naati: grandson
nana: sister
paneer: cottage cheese
parshad: offering to god
tika: blend of uncooked rice, yogurt, and vermilion smeared on
    one's forehead by elders on the day of the Tika
Tika: the most important day of the Dashain festival, during
    which elders offer "tika" to youngsters

NO LAND IS HER LAND

aaimaai: woman
ban-baas: exile

bajiyaa: rascal
chamchagiri: sycophancy
chutiya: bastard
condo: butt
daura suruwal: traditional Nepali outfit worn by men
gho: Bhutanese national costume for men
Haasnu rey: asking you to smile
khaini: tobacco
khukuri: curved Nepali knife
kira: Bhutanese national costume for women
kukkur: dog
loo hera: look at that
lyaa: Oh!
Marwari: from the Indian business community
Ram's ban-baas: the fourteen-year exile of Rama, the Hindu
    god
randi: whore
singara: fried or baked triangular pastry with savory filling
thet: alas
wah: wow

THE GURKHA'S DAUGHTER

Aayo big Gorkhali: a popular song meaning "Here come the
    brave Gurkhas"
alooko achaar: potato salad
Appa: father
Bada: uncle
Badi: aunt
bhara-kuti: toy kitchen set
Budi: wife
cheena: astrological chart
dhog: gesture of joining the palms in front of one's forehead
didi: an older sister or cousin

dosha: unfavorable alignment of stars
gauri bet: cane
gheeu: clarified butter
guniu-cholo: the traditional Nepalese outfit worn by women; a
   type of sari-blouse
havan: sacred fireplace
jaabo: useless
jardiyaa: alcoholic
kala sharpa dosha: the unfavorable alignment of stars
laurey: Gurkha soldier
Magar: a caste
Manglik: person born with the mangal dosha, usually considered unlucky
mit: name by which one summons one's fictive brother, established by the miteri ceremony
miteri: fictive kinship
mitini: name by which one summons one's fictive sister, established by the miteri ceremony
Numberee: term used by soldiers in the Gurkha regiment to
   summon others of the same year
pittu: team game played by toppling a slab of stones with
   a ball
puja: offering/prayer
Punditjee/pundit: priest
Ra-ra: a brand of noodles
safa tempo: a three-wheeled public transport vehicle
Sahib: officer
sel-roti: Nepali doughnut made of rice powder
tongba: alcohol

PASSING FANCY
Gayatri Mantra: a Vedic chant recited to remove obstacles
salaami: bonus win

THE IMMIGRANTS

Ammamama: oh my god
Baba: father
chee: expression to convey disgust
chee hou: expression to convey disdain
chutney: sauce
hapshis: blacks
kaam garne: servant
kurti: a loose shirt, shorter than the kurta